"Orange, Ms Melrose. You're painting my library orange!"

Kate glared at Steven across the table, her hazel-gold eyes sparking against the flint gray of his. "That shade happens to be peaches and cream," she informed him stiffly.

"Oh, Lord. Where did you buy something like that?" He grimaced, reaching for the pizza carton.

"I mixed it myself."

Steven's hand froze in the air, the slice of pizza midway to his mouth. His gaze seemed to soften. "Look, Kate—it's fine. I didn't mean to hurt your feelings."

"Don't be ridiculous. I'm a professional." She bit viciously down on her pizza. "I'll paint it over tomorrow. I know just the color—institutional white."

He sighed. "I *knew* your feelings were hurt. Just leave it peaches and milk or whatever."

Kate swallowed hard. "Mr. Reid—feelings have—"

"It's Steven." He leaned forward and placed his hand, warm and gentle, on hers.

"Feelings," she tried again, "have nothing to do with this!" But even as she spoke her heart was pulsing in her throat at his nearness.

"I think they do," he remarked quietly. "Quite a lot, in fact...."

Ellen James wanted a writing career ever since she won a national short story competition in high school. *Home for Love* is her first novel, and readers will enjoy its warmth and wit. Ellen lives with her husband in New Mexico, where they met—and where she plans to set her next Romance.

Home
for Love
Ellen James

Harlequin Books

TORONTO • NEW YORK • LONDON
AMSTERDAM • PARIS • SYDNEY • HAMBURG
STOCKHOLM • ATHENS • TOKYO • MILAN

ISBN 0-373-03052-5

Harlequin Romance first edition May 1990

CHAPTER ONE

THERE WAS SOMETHING special about the house. Kate's heels clicked over the scarred wooden floors; her fingers probed gently along mildewed wallpaper. She clambered up to the dusty attic, then went down to rummage in the dank basement. After she had poked about to her heart's content, she returned to the library and settled back in a window seat. San Francisco Bay shimmered far below her, tiers of rooftops sloping down to the water's edge. Kate savored the view, then turned to her briefcase. She snapped it open and took out her notepad.

The house was not stunning or imposing. It had no pretensions to grandeur, unlike so many of the places Kate decorated. And that was exactly why she felt drawn to it. This house had been built in another era—built solidly, to last. Anchored firmly to the top of the hill, it seemed more concerned with sheltering and guarding its inhabitants than with any outward display of beauty.

Kate gazed dreamily around the room, pen poised motionless over her notepad. Homely and homey all at once... but she knew she could bring out the hidden grace here, show the house that it could be beautiful. Just look at that wainscoting, and the sweep of the stairway in the hall.

Kate frowned, pushing a mahogany-red curl back from her forehead. She didn't like the impersonal way this job had been offered to her. The house belonged to a lawyer, Steven Reid, but his secretary had been the one to call and make all the arrangements. After several visits to the house Kate still found it difficult to believe that anyone even lived here. The furnishings were sparse and looked suspiciously like rental furniture. This house was definitely not a home.

"But you will be," Kate murmured. "I promise." She settled back more comfortably on the worn cushion and traced her finger along a crack in the window. As a child her one prized possession had been a dollhouse, haphazardly nailed together out of scraps of lumber but truly magnificent to her young eyes. She'd spent hours arranging and rearranging the miniature furniture, dreaming of the day she'd have a real home to love—a place far more inviting than her family's cramped, dreary little house.

Kate shook her head ruefully, pulling herself away from the memories. She was no longer a wistful child but an adult with her own interior-decorating business. And she was very proud of that business, no matter how much she sometimes had to struggle to keep herself financially afloat. She hadn't thought in a long while about owning a home of her own. This house had started the longing again, reminding her of that wonderful, shabby dollhouse she'd cherished so long ago.

But Kate didn't have time to daydream now. She began jotting down page after page of notes, all her creativity brought to life as she planned new possibilities for the house. Every time she came here she discovered something more to be done—that alcove in the hall would need its own small rug, the sink in the laundry room was badly cracked and had to be replaced. Kate wrote faster as her vision for the house deepened in color and vividness; her fingers grew cramped from their intense, eager pressure on the pen.

The knocker pounded against the front door, interrupting Kate's train of thought. She glanced at her watch, nodding in approval. The contractors she'd hired to do repairs were showing up right on schedule. She slid away from the window seat, stretching exuberantly. She'd never been quite this excited about a decorating job. Humming under her breath, she went to let the workmen inside.

Soon the house echoed with all sorts of intriguing sounds—nails screeching out of old boards, toolboxes clattering cheerfully. The house seemed to welcome all the noise and confusion, creaking comfortably at its joints. Kate was very busy the rest of the afternoon. She consulted with the carpenters and the electrician, stacked all her carpet samples in the hall and took down the musty draperies in the dining room. She badly needed her assistant, Paula, who was busy finishing the details of another decorating job.

Kate hurried through the downstairs hallway, stopping as she ran into a tangle of wires that spewed from the ceiling. She skirted a stepladder and held up a swatch of wallpaper in the light from the landing window. Peach roses or sprigs of violets? She'd better get some other samples over here before she made a decision. This narrow little hall would have to convey the welcoming nature of the house.

"What the devil is going on?" came a deep masculine voice behind Kate, somehow making itself heard above all the hammering and shouting. She swiveled and found herself looking up into angry, slate-gray eyes.

Their gaze was intense and strangely compelling. Kate fingered her wallpaper samples, unable to look away.

"Mr. Reid?" she managed. "I'm Kate Melrose—"

"Would you mind telling me what a wrecking crew is doing in my house?"

Kate gave him the smile she always kept on reserve for difficult clients. "Perhaps we can talk where it's quieter," she said, leading the way into the library. She closed the folding wooden doors. "There, that's better."

Steven Reid threw his jacket onto the lumpy sofa and loosened his tie.

"I just wanted a little paint slapped up around the place. I never said anything about demolition crews."

"I've taken on only minor repairs, Mr. Reid. Very necessary ones that shouldn't be covered up by a 'little paint.'" She allowed the slightest sarcasm to creep into her voice.

"I think I can decide what's necessary for my own house." He raked a hand through dark hair that was already thoroughly rumpled. "Look, I just got off a flight from New York. I've been staring at legal briefs for days, and all I want is a cold beer and a little peace and quiet. Do you think you could do something about that?"

Kate frowned at his autocratic tone, but held back her first biting response.

"Your fridge isn't working too well, so forget the beer. I'm having the wiring checked, though." She gave him an encouraging look, only to have him glare balefully back at her. He seemed a bit sinister, with that shadow of beard emphasizing a strongly molded jaw.

"You're an interior decorator, aren't you?" he rapped out. "I thought that's what Mrs. Adler said."

"Yes, of course."

"So you're not an electrician, and you shouldn't be fiddling with my wiring!"

"I've called in a very qualified man to do the job. I can personally vouch for him—"

"There's nothing in our contract about electricians," he said ominously. "And nothing about people tearing down my walls. May I remind you, Ms Melrose, that our agreement is a binding legal document?"

Kate folded her arms.

"I don't like the way that agreement was handled at all," she declared. "I had to sign it without even meeting you to discuss the house. Good interior design can be accomplished only after several consultations and—"

"Ms Melrose, don't lecture me. Just do something about all that racket!" he ordered. Kate clenched her teeth. There was no way she could muster up her difficult-client smile again, but she did manage a stiff nod before retreating through the folding doors. Once on the other side she allowed herself a full grimace. Why did this well-meaning house have to belong to such a cantankerous man? It simply wasn't fair.

"The client is always right," she muttered with absolutely no conviction, as she made the rounds to call off her forces.

After everyone had finally trooped out, she returned to the library prepared to be pleasantly persuasive. Instead, she found Steven Reid fast asleep, his head cushioned against the sofa back, his feet propped up on the coffee table.

Kate felt like a kettle suddenly bereft of steam. The man no longer looked combative—just tired. His black lashes were thick and straight, a sharp, definite stab of color above bold cheekbones. He breathed with a deep, even intensity, as if any snatch of sleep had to be used to full advantage. Kate tiptoed to the window seat where she'd left her briefcase. She paused at the library doors on her way out, her eyes lingering on Steven Reid. Even asleep there was a vibrancy about him, a dark attractiveness that drew her much too naturally.

Kate shook herself. It didn't seem right to stand here looking at him like this. His tall, broad-shouldered body was quite defenseless at the moment, especially with those whimsical argyle socks adorning his feet. Unable to control a smile, Kate slipped out the front door.

But she didn't stay away from the house for long. It was quite early the next morning when her little yellow Bug crawled back up the steep hill. Kate hunched patiently over the steering wheel, willing the old car onward. No matter how difficult it was to struggle up a street, she always had the promise of racing downward again. That was one of the things she liked best about San Francisco.

She turned the wheel and chugged triumphantly along the weed-choked drive of the forlorn old house. Mr. Reid's Mercedes was still parked next to the decorative pump house built like a gazebo; so much for sneaking her troops in this morning. Kate swung out of her car and stood back to observe the house. Shreds of summer fog clung to the trees around it, contributing to its air of melancholy. It had bay windows poking out in the most unexpected places, gingerbread trim in graying wood, and a Queen Anne tower worn like a party hat long after the celebration was over. Kate moved a step closer. She'd give the house some confidence with a coat of sunny yellow paint—and coconut-cream paint for the trim, of course. She nodded in satisfaction. Armed with her briefcase, she marched up the brick steps of the porch and lifted the tarnished brass knocker.

There was no answer after several knocks. She rummaged in her briefcase and took out the key Mr. Reid's secretary had given her.

"Hello?" She poked her head inside the door. When again there was no answer, she headed for the window seat in the library. She glanced disapprovingly at the half-eaten bowl of potato chips on the coffee table. Then, humming to herself, she pulled out her notepad and began jotting down some reminders. She wanted the carpenters to build a bookshelf for the tower room, curved to fit snugly against the round wall. And the mahogany armoire she'd special-ordered would be delivered this week; perhaps it would look best in the corner bedroom.

"Do you always wander into people's houses uninvited, Ms Melrose?"

Kate turned and found herself blushing uncomfortably. Steven Reid was standing there dripping wet in the doorway, with nothing but a towel wrapped around his waist. Kate averted her eyes quickly from the tangled mat of hair on his broad chest. But the strong, powerful lines of his body were already etched into her mind. She swallowed hard.

"Ah . . . good morning, Mr. Reid."

"I thought I told you not to come back," he said brusquely.

"Well, no, we didn't get that far yesterday. But don't mind me. I'll just get to work while you, uh, go on with whatever."

"You're not supposed to be doing any work," he said.

"Mr. Reid, about our discussion yesterday—"

"I don't recall any discussion. You're going to stop ripping my house apart. That's all." As he spoke, his eyes traveled over her with frowning thoroughness. He examined her swept-up auburn hair, her hazel eyes, the faint but stubborn smattering of freckles across her nose. It was impossible to tell from his expression whether or not she had passed inspection. She concentrated on searching through her briefcase.

"Now, why don't we just sit down with a cup of tea and talk this over," she said in a reasonable tone. "Peppermint's the best . . . Here's some."

Steven glanced skeptically from her briefcase to the tea bags she was holding up, then back at her briefcase. A smile tugged at the corner of his mouth.

"No, thanks," he said dryly. "I'll stick to strong black coffee."

"Caffeine," she warned. Steven ignored her, turning back into the hallway. Kate hurried after him. He pulled up so abruptly that she almost bumped against him. She breathed a heady whiff of clean wet skin and sea-fresh soap before she backed away. She was wearing heels, but in bare feet he still towered over her.

"Look what you've done," he muttered, gesturing at clumps of wires and chunks of plasterboard.

"I told you, these are just minor repairs."

"They don't look minor." He peered at the walls as if he expected them to come tumbling down at any moment. "Well, good day, Ms Melrose. You can settle up your account with Mrs. Adler. Just be glad I'm not suing for damages."

Kate stood very still, feeling stunned. She had never, ever been fired from a job before. This simply could not be happening. She wouldn't *allow* it to happen!

She was right beside Steven when he reached the upstairs landing.

"Mr. Reid, we have an agreement! You said yourself that it's a binding document—"

"Only if both parties abide by the terms. You've gone way too far."

"Mr. Reid—"

"I'm going to finish my shower now. Do you intend to follow me there, too?"

"Of course not," she said stiffly, watching his muscular calves until they disappeared around the corner.

Good legs shouldn't be wasted on such a man. He was impossible. Kate sank down on the first step, drawing up her knees. Steven Reid made her feel as if all her years of hard work were on the line here. As long as she could remember, she had been dreaming, planning, struggling to make Melrose Designs a success. She couldn't afford to lose this job—and not just for financial reasons. The house needed her. That was all there was to it.

When Steven came downstairs again, this time fully clothed in well-tailored slacks and a tweed jacket, Kate was in the kitchen with her tea bags. She had found two mugs and a jar of instant coffee in the bare cupboards. Steven gazed at her sardonically. He looked vibrant with energy now, strong jaw freshly shaven and his thick dark hair only slightly repressed by dampness from the shower.

"You must like goodbyes, Ms Melrose," he said. She watched in consternation as he twisted the lid from a jar of olives.

"Is that what you're having for breakfast?" she asked.

"That and the strongest coffee known to mankind. Any comment?"

"A carton of yogurt would be good. Doesn't take any time to prepare, and it has lots of protein."

Steven popped an olive into his mouth and reached for a battered pan. He started filling it with water.

"Wonderful, Ms Melrose. I'll keep your homemaking tips in mind. Goodbye."

She grabbed the pan from him and finished filling it at the leaky faucet.

"I really do believe we can clear up this misunderstanding," she told him firmly. "When I consulted with your Mrs. Adler, she told me to use my own judgment on the repair work. She said . . ." Kate paused for accusatory emphasis. "She said you weren't even interested in discussing the details."

Steven struck a match and lit one of the stove burners. He took the pan back from Kate.

"I think tearing the walls down constitutes more than a detail."

"Yes, but if you don't even *care* about the house—"

"I bought the damn thing, didn't I?"

"Well, yes—"

"Fine. Then we've settled everything. Good*bye*, Ms Melrose." He chomped down on another olive. Kate sat on one of the battered kitchen chairs and stared at him.

"You have some bread that's not too stale," she remarked. "Toasted in the oven it wouldn't be bad at all."

Steven straddled the chair across from her.

"Plying me with food isn't going to work, Ms Melrose."

"I'll keep the repairs to a minimum. Now, before you say anything, just hear me out. I think it *is* important to finish what I've started with the wiring. Beyond that, there's just one section of the roof that can't be neglected, and—"

"Ms Melrose—"

"A bit of carpentry and one room to be replastered. That's all. And here's the good part. I will make sure— *absolutely* sure—that everyone is gone whenever you're here. All you have to do is tell me when to clear out. Fair enough?"

The water was boiling. Steven dumped an alarming amount of coffee into his mug, swirling hot water on top of it. He glanced at Kate's mug, hesitated, and then with a beleaguered sigh poured some over her tea bag.

"I'll admit you're stubborn. But the answer is still no. Just the way it was in the beginning."

Kate shook her head emphatically. "In the beginning you hired me. At least your Mrs. Adler did. I just can't understand why you've suddenly changed your mind."

"Because I suddenly had my house falling down around my ears."

Kate's hazel-gold eyes sparked against the gray flint of Steven's. "Mr. Reid. Give me one reason, just one reason why you wouldn't want essential repairs to be made."

He scowled at her for a long moment without saying anything. No one had ever regarded her with such patent disgust before. She lifted her chin. Steven Reid was definitely not good for the ego.

"I don't even know why I bought the place," he muttered at last. "I've only moved here temporarily from New York. I'll probably just have to sell it again."

"There must be a reason you bought it," she insisted.

He shrugged as he spoke. "I drove by it once, just by accident. All that scraggly grass and peeling paint, and the shingles dropping off. After that, I came by every day for a month. It got to be damned inconvenient. I had to do something about it."

"Well—"

"Look, Ms Melrose, I'm handling a big merger right now. I don't need all this aggravation."

"And you won't have any, I promise," she said earnestly. "You'll never even know I was here."

He drank his coffee, still frowning at her over the rim of his mug. Then he plunked the mug down on the table.

"Show me what you intend to do," he said so suddenly that Kate started and sloshed tea out of her cup. She recovered quickly and led him to the small sun room, which was badly in need of work. Then she took him to the attic, where she discoursed on the value of minor patching now to avoid major flooding later.

"Enough!" Steven protested. "Look . . . all right, I accept the roof job. And maybe the other repairs—if I know I can come home at night and not find a wall or two missing."

"You have my word," she told him fervently, as her nose began to itch from all the dust and grime in the attic. She tried to fish casually in her pocket for a tissue, only to have a large plaid handkerchief thrust at her just in time for her sneeze.

"Thank you." She peered over the vivid red-and-green cloth, wondering if it had actually materialized from somewhere inside that subdued tweed jacket. She glanced surreptitiously at Steven's feet; they were hidden in low-key but expensive loafers and it was impossible to tell if he was wearing fanciful argyle socks today.

Her gaze traveled upward again to lock with those sea-gray eyes. The attic suddenly seemed too intimate a place to be conducting a business transaction. Perhaps it was the lowness of the ceiling, or the presence of rotting boxes and chests that bespoke old memories. Kate folded the bandanna-sized handkerchief and tried cramming it into one of her strictly decorative pockets.

"I'll return this to you." She advanced cautiously toward the trapdoor. "What is all this up here?" she asked, brushing a film of dirt from the top of one of the boxes.

"I haven't had a chance to investigate. I think I'll just toss it all out."

"Oh, no, don't do that!" she exclaimed. "You have to find out what's inside first. If you don't you'll always wonder what treasures you missed."

"No. *You'll* always wonder, Ms Melrose," came his dry response as he disappeared down through the trapdoor. Kate certainly did not like advancing rear view first down the ladder, and turned around to face him again as soon as possible.

"Now, just tell me when you want me out of here today," she said in her most agreeable tone.

"You're in luck. I won't be back from the office until late tonight."

"Wonderful! I mean—I'll stick to my part of the agreement. And you won't regret this, Mr. Reid. You really won't."

He gave her a look that showed he was already regretting it. Downstairs again he picked up his briefcase.

"So long, Ms Melrose."

"You might as well call me Kate," she said brightly.

He gave the idea a frown, but after a moment shrugged. "Goodbye...Kate."

There was absolutely no reason her pulse should have quickened when he said her name. He'd pushed it out of his mouth very grudgingly, in fact.

She was relieved when a moment later the Mercedes rolled down the drive. Kate scrambled to the phone and called her workers back on duty. Then she settled herself in the window seat to wait for them and to savor her victory.

She allowed herself the luxury of slipping off her shoes and tucking her legs up. As a child she would have loved a window seat like this, a special spot for herself. She was the middle child in a family of seven, and private space had been an unknown commodity. Kate's only retreat was to curl up next to her dollhouse. Even so her younger sisters were always losing the little sofas, chairs and beds Kate had fashioned from bits of cardboard.

She smiled, remembering. Her life had certainly changed. She'd worked her way through art school, studying and sketching for her classes late at night and on weekends. She hadn't enjoyed much of a social life, but she'd graduated with honors. Nothing could daunt her after that, not even the job selling floor tile. She simply made herself an expert on tiles and then moved on. Now, at twenty-five, she had her own business. She could be proud of her accomplishments, despite the skepticism of Steven Reid.

She wasn't looking forward to working with him. Not at all. Yet he was a puzzle to her. He seemed more the type to choose a luxury town house than a place that needed so much love and care. He certainly looked the image of a successful lawyer.

Kate fingered a corner of the handkerchief trailing out of her pocket. After a moment's hesitation she brought it up to her face and inhaled tentatively.

The handkerchief smelled of pine after-shave, clean, brisk and masculine. Kate took a deep breath.

She opened her eyes wide. What was she doing? She stuffed the handkerchief unceremoniously back into her pocket. Swinging her legs down, she slipped her feet into her pumps where they belonged. She was determined about one thing. Steven Reid or no Steven Reid, this house was going to be the best work of her career.

CHAPTER TWO

Soon afterward Kate's assistant, Paula, arrived on the job, her six-foot teenage brother, Max, in tow. The two of them busied themselves with paintbrushes and rollers in the library. Kate watched for a moment, admiring the smooth, meticulous strokes of Paula's brush. As usual Paula was studious about her work. Max's habits were slapdash in comparison, his blond hair falling into his face. But this brother-and-sister team was part of what made Melrose Designs so special. "The personal touch"—that was how Kate advertised, and she stuck by her motto. She herself always looked forward to completing the details of a job. She was an expert at wallpapering difficult corners and varnishing intricate moldings. Being so self-sufficient was an advantage, allowing Kate to make competitive bids against larger decorating firms that hired out all their physical labor.

But business and financial motives played no part in Kate's eagerness to work on Steven's house; the place reached her emotions in a much deeper way. She was going to patch and mend many of its injuries herself, because no one else would care about them as much as she did. Just wait until she started on the wainscoting!

For today, however, other needs of the house called first. Kate left the carpenters and roofers under Paula's supervision and took off to the shops of Union Street.

She poked about happily for hours, looking for the right things to grace Steven's empty rooms. She found two intricate, colorful embroideries for the upstairs hallway, along with baskets in three different sizes for the kitchen. And she doubted that Steven had a wok, so she bought him one of those, too.

Kate's Bug began to overflow with bundles. She managed to rope a chair and a chest of drawers to the roof, but finally ran out of space. Her little car toiled up McClary Hill like an overladen mule just as twilight was drifting down. By now the house was deserted, all the workers gone. Kate savored this solitude, her own special time to be creative. She was her own boss and didn't have to follow someone else's rigid schedule.

The house surrounded her with a lonely but comfortable gloom as she arranged her purchases. A deep sense of contentment grew inside her, a feeling that was the house's unique gift to her. She pushed stray wisps of hair away from her face and phoned out for pizza. Afterward she gravitated to the sun room, carrying the small rattan chair she'd bought at one of her favorite shops, the exotic Malaysian Star. She placed the chair in a corner, then stepped back and smiled. She'd known it would look perfect there. It was her best find of the day.

Kate gazed out the window, a swirl of fog softening the city lights below her. She took a plaster scraper and began the pleasurable task of chipping some hardened dirt away from the frame. The perfect shade of paint for this room would be "adobe rose," no doubt about it. And she'd use blinds instead of curtains. Already she could picture how the sun would look slanting through them.

The front door creaked open forcefully, then banged shut again. Footsteps strode down the hall and they did not sound pleased. A moment later Steven's tall body filled the doorway. Kate stared at him, scraper poised in her hand.

"Oh, no!" she wailed. "You can't be here yet."

"Ms Melrose, you swore to me—"

"Kate."

"You swore I'd have some peace and quiet tonight."

"I know, I know. I did make sure everyone else would be gone. But you said you'd be home late."

"It *is* late."

She squinted at her watch. "Not that late," she murmured hopefully.

"Exactly what is your definition of late?" He pried a sticky newspaper away from his foot.

"Well...not this early. Later than this. Much later. Then it would really be late."

He glared at her and she moved hastily away from the window. "Believe me, this won't happen again," she declared, then tripped over a bucket of rags and landed in Steven's arms.

She caught her breath as she swayed against him. Steven's face was very close to hers, eyes a deep gray under his definite brows. The dark shadow of beard emphasized his clean, healthy skin. His tie was loosened, hanging at a rakish angle. With the top two buttons of his shirt undone, Kate could see a hint of his curling mat of chest hair. She drew away, her breath coming unevenly.

"Are you always this graceful?" he asked, with a glint of humor.

"Believe it or not, I took ballet lessons when I was a little girl. But I had the biggest feet in my class."

"They look fine now," he said. Kate felt his gaze on her maroon pumps. Then he took hold of her hand and examined its small, square shape. He stroked the inside of her wrist, very lightly and very gently, with a slight frown, as if he didn't quite know why he was doing this. Kate's pulse throbbed. She snatched her hand away—or maybe he dropped it abruptly, it was hard to tell.

"I'll be out of here in thirty seconds," she said. "Everything is coming along marvelously, by the way. It's a good, sound house—but of course you knew that. Otherwise you wouldn't have bought it."

"I didn't know a thing about the construction," he said gruffly. "I could have been buying a house made out of cardboard, for all I knew."

Kate stared at him in surprise. "You can't be serious. Why, that's like saying—it's like saying—"

"It's like saying I'm a damned fool. Now we've established that, do you think we can get on with life?"

"I'm sorry," she said. "I didn't mean to imply anything. I'll be gone in ten seconds." She popped into the library and picked up her briefcase. Steven followed, leaning in the doorway to watch her. She was uncomfortably aware of her rumpled skirt and dusty blouse. But Steven's gaze swept away from her to the sheet-draped sofa.

"What have you been doing in here?" he asked, yanking the sheet away.

"Painting. Don't you think the color is going to be wonderful?" She gestured at a wall that was almost finished. "And of course we covered the furniture even though it is atrocious. I think you'll be so pleased with the new things I have in mind."

"Ms Melrose!"

"Kate, remember? Of course, I could just keep calling you Mr. Reid if you prefer—"

"I don't care what you call me. Just don't touch this couch."

"You can't be serious!" she protested. "It's outrageous. It'll spoil the whole room. I mean, *look* at it—"

"I like it, Ms Melrose. Kate. It's very comfortable and it's just the right length."

"I can get you a long couch. Extra long. Made to order, even."

"I don't want another couch. I want this one. Do you understand?"

She sighed explosively. "I think we should discuss this later."

"Discussion closed, now and forever."

"All right, all right," she grumbled, eyeing the sofa. She wouldn't mind taking a machete to those cushions.

"I don't think I trust you," Steven said slowly.

"Don't be ridiculous. It's your sofa, your house. The customer...the customer is always right," she muttered.

Steven glanced at her quizzically. Just then the knocker rapped at the front door. "Who the devil can that be?" he asked, rubbing his neck. "There's enough going on here already."

"Uh, well, Steven," Kate said hesitantly. "You see, I didn't expect you back yet and—" the knocker banged again "—I ordered pizza," she wound up. She set down her briefcase and slipped past him to the front door. A moment later she returned, bearing a large box.

"Mushrooms, olives and extra cheese," she announced. "On a whole-wheat crust. Look, just take this as an apology for the fact that I didn't keep my end of the bargain. After today you won't even know I exist."

He glanced around at the half-painted walls and the colorful sheets strewn about. "You don't seem like the type of woman who fades into the woodwork," he said.

"I promise to disappear. Right now." She prodded the box into his hands. "I'll be out of here in five seconds."

"Kate..." He sighed. "Just put two plates on the table, will you? I'll hunt up something to drink."

She led the way into the kitchen, holding the swinging door open for him as he came through with the box.

"Thank you," he said dryly.

"You're welcome." Kate washed her hands and took a long, enjoyable time patting them dry on one of the linen towels she'd bought that day. Then she hunted through the cupboards, where she found only a couple of plastic plates; she'd have to do something about that. Steven uncorked a bottle of wine and located two cheap wineglasses. Kate sat across from him, feet hooked around her chair legs, and tore off a piece of pizza.

"It's good," she said encouragingly. "Don't you think so?"

He read the lid of the box. "'Penelope's Pizza Parlor.' Is this for real?"

"Of course. It's the best in town, from a little place in North Beach. Very nourishing, too. Don't tell me you've never had any before."

"Whole wheat," he said disparagingly, but a moment later added, "Not too bad."

Kate sat back in triumph. Now and then Steven Reid was almost human. If only she could convince him to get rid of that lumpy sofa, with its dismal brown cushions.

But she'd have to bide her time. After all, she'd dealt before with clients who hung on unreasonably to favorite pieces of furniture. She'd always been able to wean them. She could do the same thing with Steven when the time was right.

She smiled confidently across at him and felt a quiver down her spine when he actually smiled back. He had a full, mobile mouth that was somehow in keeping with the sharp and vigorous planes of his face. She liked the way his hair sprang back from his high, well-molded forehead.

Kate gulped some wine and started coughing. She pushed her glass away. Wine on top of paint fumes could make a person feel heady like this.

"You know, you really ought to improve your diet," she declared. "I mean, all you have in the fridge is stale bread—*white* bread—and some very suspect mayonnaise. Actually, you don't have the mayonnaise anymore. I did you a favor and threw it out."

Steven's slice of pizza froze in the air midway to his mouth. "The inside of my refrigerator doesn't need redecorating."

"Well, of course not. It has to go entirely. I already have ideas for a new model. It's going to take some searching around, but I'll find what I want. Something with rounded edges—old-fashioned, you know, in keeping with the spirit of the house."

Steven chomped down viciously on his pizza. "The fridge stays," he said.

"You know, I've considered that, too. With a little refurbishing, it could be very decorative. I could convert it to a storage area. And can't you just see a couple of trailing plants on top of it? Maybe a fern—"

"No plants. I want it plugged into the wall, and I want it stocked with rotten mayonnaise."

Kate set down her pizza and struggled to maintain a reasonable tone. "I always try to stay true to my clients' wishes, of course. It's just that I didn't know you really *had* any specific ideas for the house. How do you envision the overall scheme?"

"I don't. I told you, I just want a little paint slapped up. Only I was thinking more in terms of white."

"White paint?" Kate asked faintly.

"What else?"

"Lavender, honey, robin's-egg blue—"

"Orange. You're painting my library orange!"

They glared at each other across the table.

"That shade happens to be 'peaches-and-cream,'" Kate informed him stiffly.

"Oh, Lord. Where did you buy something like that?"

"I mixed it myself."

His gaze seemed to soften. "Look, Kate—it's fine."

"If you don't like it, just say so."

"I didn't mean to hurt your feelings."

"Don't be ridiculous. I'm a professional."

"Professionals can be just as susceptible to wounded feelings as other people," he pointed out.

"I'll paint it over. I know just the color. 'Institutional white.' I think you'll like that." She chewed her pizza vigorously.

"I *knew* your feelings were hurt. Just leave it peaches-and-milk, or whatever."

"Mr. Reid—"

"Steven."

"Let me explain to you one more time that feelings have absolutely nothing to do with this!"

"I think they do," he remarked. "Quite a lot, in fact. You're taking everything personally. Why not just admit it? Then we can get on with the job."

She took a deep breath.

"All you have to do is tell me what you want done with the house. I'll be more than happy to comply."

"I don't know what I want," he said. "If I did, you wouldn't be here in the first place."

"White paint. That's it? That's your only opinion? I should have saved the mayonnaise. I could have slapped that on a few walls."

They ate the rest of the pizza in stubborn silence. Afterward Kate stuffed the empty box into the trash and filled the sink with water.

"You need a drain board," she said. Steven didn't answer. The silence between them vibrated with a sultry tension as they stood side by side at the sink. Kate's hands moved over the dishes in the sudsy water; Steven took the dishes from her, rinsed them and dried them with a paper towel. Her heart was pulsing in her throat at his nearness.

Steven's hand slid into the warm, soapy water. His fingers bumped gently against hers and he turned toward her. She parted her lips to protest, but no words would come out. She couldn't make herself step away from him. There was a sweet, heavy expectancy in her limbs.

His lips moved over her temple, brushed the line where her hair grew from a widow's peak.

"Lovely," he murmured, his voice husky. "You're lovely, Kate." He brought her close to him—slowly, inexorably. His mouth descended to cover hers.

It was not a demanding kiss. It wasn't hurried. Steven made a leisurely exploration, discovering each subtle contour of her lips. His touch was like warm, golden honey spreading through her. It tantalized her, teased with its gentleness. Her fingers reached out to twine with his in the water.

Now he bent his head to her throat, tasting her bare skin. When he returned to her mouth his lips were harder, seeking a deeper response from her.

She felt suddenly frightened, the warmth inside her fanning into a flame. What was she doing?

"No!" The word came out in a strangled cry. She struggled away from him, cradling her wet hand against her body.

"Look, Kate..." he began, but she backed away from him. She didn't want to talk about it. Surely it was bad enough that this had happened at all.

"I'm going," she said shakily. "I'll keep to my promise. From now on...from now on you won't even see me." She ran to the hall, grabbed up her briefcase and fled out the door.

Her cheeks burned with confusion even in the cool night air. Nothing seemed familiar to her anymore; her hands fumbled with the car keys, and she nearly flooded the Bug's engine when she started it up. She was relieved to make it out the drive and down McClary Hill. She drove across town, pushing the little car as fast as it would go.

Kate turned onto her own street of restored Victorian row houses. They rose in the fog like gaunt, fussy old ladies. She was glad to see them, for her heart was still beating a wild tattoo. She managed to park at the curb, then hurried up the steps of the house where she lived. It had been converted into three apartments. Her own was on the top floor, and she was immensely relieved to reach it. She needed a safe harbor to calm herself and straighten out her emotions.

She extracted a tea bag from her briefcase and heated some water in the kitchen. A few moments later she was able to sink gratefully into her rocking chair, a turn-of-the-century piece, with faded needlepoint cushions. She rocked fiercely and sipped her tea.

All right. She was physically attracted to Steven. Very much so. That was perfectly normal; she was a young, healthy woman. And he had kissed her, tenderly and completely.

Kate sprang up and the rocker nearly went over backward. She pressed her forehead against the cool glass of the window, her brain befuddled with a fog all its own. She had to decide how she was going to handle this. She'd never been kissed by a client before. *No one* had ever kissed her like that.

She had to admit she wasn't very experienced with this sort of thing. She'd always been too busy with her career to develop a serious relationship with a man. And now she had her own business, her own life. She was independent and happy. She wanted to keep things exactly that way. Certainly she wasn't going to pursue what had happened tonight. She didn't need a man intruding on her hard-won independence. Especially not a dangerous man like Steven Reid. A man like that could change a woman's life forever.

Kate wouldn't give him the opportunity. She'd keep her promise and stay well out of his path. She'd finish her work on the house and never see him again.

She sank down into the rocker again and picked up her cup. But peppermint tea wasn't comforting her tonight. She'd always been able to count on peppermint tea.

Now it was just growing cold in the cup. This was a very bad sign indeed.

CHAPTER THREE

KATE BURROWED DEEPER under her pillow, trying to ignore the telephone jangling on her bedside table. She had tossed restlessly most of the night, dreaming that she was in Steven's arms. She wasn't ready to face the world yet, but the telephone wouldn't stop ringing. Kate was forced to emerge.

"Hello?" she croaked into the receiver, rubbing her eyes against early-morning sunlight.

"Ms Melrose, this is Florence Adler," came the dry, efficient voice of Steven's secretary. "I'm calling to arrange an appointment for you with Mr. Reid. He would like you to meet him at Lendal's this afternoon at precisely four-twenty. Shall I put you down in the book?"

"Wait a minute," Kate sputtered, struggling away from a tangle of sheet and blanket. "I mean—please, could you tell me what this is all about?"

"Mr. Reid did not provide me with any details on the matter," the secretary said in a hushed voice, as if Kate had just asked her to divulge state secrets. "I am sure, however, that Mr. Reid would not request this meeting unless it were essential. He is a very busy man."

Kate sighed, her eyes wide open now. "What time did you say?"

"Four-twenty sharp. Shall I give you detailed instructions to the restaurant? You turn south on—"

"That's fine, Mrs. Adler," Kate interrupted. "I'll find it. Yes, yes, I'll be there. You can even write my name down in ink." Disgruntled, she hung up the phone. Avoiding Steven would be difficult with Mrs. Adler calling up to arrange appointments. And why not four o'clock, or four-thirty? Who on earth made appointments at four-twenty?

Kate dressed, then ate her breakfast without appetite. Paula arrived a short while later to discuss business.

"Mrs. Cleeve has decided to go Japanese all the way," she exclaimed as soon as she was inside the door. "Can you believe it, after she had us do her entire house in French Provincial? Now she's determined to have nothing but cushions. I mean it, Kate! Literally nothing but cushions and pillows. That means all her tables can't be higher than sixteen inches! What am I supposed to do with the ones we ordered? Chop off their legs?" Paula sounded on the verge of tears. Her brown eyes were big and dark in her slender face; her shining blond hair swung in two smooth arcs toward her chin. She looked especially young today and Kate had to resist the urge to protect her. Paula was unsure of her own abilities, but she had enough talent to become a full partner in the business someday.

"All right, calm down," Kate said in her most authoritative yet soothing voice. "Everything will be just fine."

"But, Kate, she's insisting that it's all our fault, the tables being too tall! She won't pay the balance on her account."

Kate chewed the tip of her pen. This wasn't good news, especially after the money she'd spent lately on Steven's house. It was her practice to give clients a

complete estimate of what a job would cost, including
everything from the price of new draperies to the fee for
her own time and expertise. She generally requested
one-half of this amount in advance, an arrangement
that usually gave her satisfactory working capital until
the job was completed. But Steven's house was different. It had needs she could not even have guessed at in
the beginning, needs she could learn only as she ab-
sorbed more of the house's shy yet gracious spirit. This
meant she was using up Steven's deposit money much
faster than she'd expected.

Kate set down her pen, reminding herself firmly that
all her purchases and repairs so far had been absolutely
necessary. Somehow everything would work out. She
turned back to her assistant. "Just relax. I know you
can take care of Mrs. Cleeve, Paula. And we agreed you
should have more responsibility, right?"

"Yes, but not *this* much! Mrs. Cleeve's place has
twenty rooms. It's the biggest account we've ever had,
and I'm afraid we're going to lose it!"

"Don't talk like that. You have to have a positive attitude to survive in this business," Kate said.

Paula took a deep breath, then let the air out slowly
through pursed lips. She sounded like a balloon deflat-
ing.

"I don't think having a positive attitude is enough,
Kate. The problem is, you're becoming obsessed with
that Reid house and leaving me in the lurch with Mrs.
Cleeve."

Paula was right, unfortunately. Kate wasn't interested in decorating any other house but Steven's right
now. She loved that old place; it was as simple as that.

"Look," she said to Paula, "take Mrs. Cleeve over
to Applebee's and buy her a short table or two. Let her

live with them for a few days, and she's bound to reconsider.''

"But, Kate—"

"Don't worry. I'll come by tonight and have a talk with her."

"You promise, Kate?"

"I promise. Now, we'd both better get busy. I'm going straight up to McClary Hill."

Even working at the house did not help Kate, however. Her sense of contentment was gone, replaced by a restless unease. The atmosphere was still charged after the way Steven had kissed her last night. By the time she had to leave for her appointment with him, Kate's insides had twisted into one big, apprehensive knot.

Lendal's Restaurant, located deep among the skyscrapers of the financial district, was famous for the high-powered business deals transacted over its tables. The decor had been borrowed from San Francisco's late-nineteenth century Bonanza era. Kate glanced around at the mirrors framed in gilt, the walls covered in maroon satin, the lush ferns cascading from marble pedestals. All the patrons, men and women, wore somber business suits. Kate nonchalantly straightened the collar of her brightly flowered shirt and tucked one hand into the pocket of her corduroy jeans, clutching her briefcase with the other. She felt out of place here, but she certainly wasn't going to show it.

Then she saw Steven. He was just rising from a table in a leather-upholstered booth, shaking hands with two men outfitted in drab suits. But there was nothing drab about Steven. His tweed jacket had a casual flair, and his vigorous good looks hinted at the untamed. As the two men walked away, Steven turned to scan the restaurant. His eyes locked with Kate's, and suddenly she seemed to have forgotten how to walk across a room. Steven wasn't any help; he just stood there, looking at her intently without smiling or even nodding an acknowledgment. At last Kate was able to put one foot in front of the other, propelling herself toward him.

"Hello, Steven," she said as breezily as possible.

"Thank you for coming, Kate," he answered, his tone formal. "I had a business meeting here, and thought it might be a good idea if you and I met here, as well—on neutral ground." Steven stood beside her as she slid into the booth, his hand brushing her shoulder. Kate was left with a warm, tingling sensation.

Steven sat down across from her. "Would you like something to eat or drink?" he asked, the gravity of his expression relaxing slightly as he watched her.

"I'll have a cranberry juice, thank you, with a slice of orange."

Steven's expression relaxed still further, almost into a smile, and he ordered two cranberry juices with orange slices. Kate pulled her notepad from her briefcase, ready with her pen. But Steven leaned back against the rich leather of his seat, apparently in no hurry to explain the purpose of the meeting. Kate found herself gazing at his generous, expressive mouth, her body remembering that kiss.

"I bought something for the house on my way over here today," Steven said.

"Oh?" Kate answered distractedly, hanging on to her notepad.

"Yes. I'd like to show it to you." He produced a roll of paper from the seat beside him and spread it out on the table in front of Kate.

It was a print of Monet's *Red Boats at Argenteuil*. She contemplated the subtle, shimmering contrasts of water and sky, the sailboats heading lazily out from the wharves. After a long moment she looked up and gave Steven a beneficent smile. The knot inside her was slowly beginning to unravel.

"This is wonderful. I can have it framed—and I think one of the upstairs rooms would be perfect for it."

"Good," he said, rolling it up again.

"I didn't know you were interested in art."

"Why does that surprise you?" he asked.

"I don't know. The problem is, I don't really know you at all." She found herself gazing at his mouth again, and had to avert her eyes. "I mean, I do try to have an idea of my clients' personalities. The house should reflect *you* . . ." Kate paused, forehead wrinkled in perplexity.

"I'm glad you find the idea so appealing," he said dryly.

"You don't understand. It's just that I don't have you figured out yet. Are you the mayonnaise-on-the-walls type, or Monet-on-the-walls?"

He gave her a slow grin. "Maybe I'm both. Maybe people aren't as easy to catalog as wallpaper samples."

"I'm not trying to *catalog* you," she protested. "I'm just trying to do my job. And I can't do it if you won't give me at least a little insight about yourself. Why don't you tell me about your taste in art?"

"Good Lord, that's not something you just spit out for social conversation. Show me a painting. I'll tell you if I like it."

Why did everything have to be so difficult with this man? She tried again. "Well, you must know if you hate abstract art, or if impressionism is your favorite, or baroque . . ."

"I'm open to anything."

Kate drew a jagged little line across her pad. First he wanted plain white walls, now he was "open to anything!"

"All right," she said. "Let's narrow that down a bit. What sort of house did you grow up in? What did you like about it? What didn't you like?"

He settled back with a frosted glass of cranberry juice, his gray eyes enigmatic. But at last he began, "It was a big, rambling, drafty old house in Vermont. Ever been to Vermont?"

"No..."

"I think you'd like it. The mountains, all that snow. We used to go sledding every winter, straight down the hill from our back door."

"We? How many of you?"

"Four brothers and my sister, Allie."

"I come from a big family, myself!" Kate exclaimed. "With me it's three sisters and three brothers. I'm sandwiched right in the middle. How about you?"

"Tail end of the bunch, except for Allie."

"That poor girl," Kate murmured. "Five big brothers to torment her!"

"You know the territory, I see."

"You'd better believe it," she said. "Never being able to use the bathroom when you want to. Your sisters always wearing your favorite clothes."

"How about four brothers beating up on you at once?" he asked. "Driving the old Chevy that was good enough for them, so why shouldn't it be good enough for you?"

Kate nodded, laughing. "Never having your own room or a private conversation on the phone. Oh, and those awful trips to the grocery store—buying everything in the jumbo size."

"I know. Trying to pretend you don't belong to that crazed-looking lady who has three carts lined up at the checkout stand."

They were both laughing now, so hard that they drew stares from other booths. Kate's sides began to hurt. She wiped her eyes with the big red-and-green bandanna she'd pulled from one of her pockets. She blinked down at it.

"I forgot to give this back to you, and now I've used it again."

"Keep it," Steven said. "You can give it back... whenever."

"Thanks."

There was suddenly a silence between them, strained and uncomfortable. Kate sipped her juice, but couldn't think of a thing to say.

"Why did you decide to be an interior designer?" Steven asked.

"It's something I've always wanted, I suppose. Even when I was five years old—can you believe it? The rest of my family... well, my mother just didn't have time to make our home pretty. I was the one trying to figure out how to hang the curtains better, or how to hide that awful spot on the carpet." She stopped, hesitant to reveal too much about herself. "So... why did you decide to become a lawyer?" she countered.

He gazed at her thoughtfully, taking a moment to answer.

"I wasn't like you—knowing what I wanted from the very beginning. I was a pretty wild kid, I guess. Studying law gave a direction to my life I'd never had before." He propped his elbows on the table; now he seemed to be talking more to himself than to her. "I saw a way to change things, to make a difference. But it's been too easy to get caught up with the business side of it all. The past few days I've been thinking about re-ordering my priorities. When I wrap things up in San Francisco, maybe I can get back to the grass-roots level. That's where the excitement is.''

Kate listened to the enthusiasm in his voice. She wanted to ask him more about his plans, but she didn't like the part about wrapping things up here. Her reaction was disturbing. She ought to feel relieved that he might be leaving.

''I'll probably send you off to sleep with all this talk,'' he said gruffly.

''Oh, no!'' she exclaimed. ''It's not that. It's just . . . I'm the one taking your time.'' She dropped her notepad back into her briefcase, trying to act as busi-nesslike as possible. ''You probably have another meeting to go to. Mrs. Adler said you were very busy—''

''Kate, you know we have to talk about it. Our kiss last night.'' He said the words so matter-of-factly. Kate stiffened.

''Really, Steven, there's nothing to talk about. Not a thing.'' She clutched her briefcase.

''I think there is.'' He ran a hand over the veneer of the tabletop. ''I wanted to apologize for what hap-pened. It was…a mistake. I think we both realize that.''

Kate nibbled her lip. He didn't have to be *quite* so apologetic. But he was right; she did agree that the whole thing had been a mistake.

''I'm sure it won't happen again,'' she said. ''It was unprofessional, to say the least.''

''I'm glad you see it the same way,'' he remarked.

''Well, it's never a good idea to get involved with a business associate.'' Kate relaxed her hold on the briefcase. "Besides, I enjoy my life just the way it is. I'm not looking to get involved with anyone. I'm a very independent person."

"So I've noticed," he said wryly.

"A woman has to be," she declared. "Take my mother, for instance. She adored my father, but he was so domineering. He tried to manage her, just like she was one of the kids. Even now she can't see what he did to her."

"I take it he couldn't manage *you* too well."

"We had our differences," Kate admitted. "But he did care for me. I remember him staying up late one Christmas Eve to finish building a dollhouse, which became very special to me. I still have it, in fact, stored away in my closet."

Steven smiled at her. She felt a pleasurable warmth seeping through her. She liked being able to speak so frankly with him.

"So...I didn't want you to have any bad feelings about last night," he said.

"Oh, I don't. Not anymore. I'm glad we cleared the air. I really am."

"It won't happen again."

"No. Of course not."

They gazed at each other. Steven's eyes looked almost blue now, very clear and deep. Kate glanced hurriedly at her watch.

"Um, I think I'd better be going now," she said.

Both of them stood up at the same time. Steven paid the tab and escorted Kate outside. He started hailing a taxi.

"Don't you have your car?" Kate asked.

"In the shop for maintenance."

Kate shrugged. Her own car only went into the shop for emergency repairs, never anything so prosaic as maintenance. She waved the taxi on.

"I'm giving you a ride," she announced. "No, don't argue with me. Anywhere you'd like to go." She was feeling very kind toward him now that everything was straightened out between them.

"Actually, I have to go back up to the house," Steven told her. "I'm due at a fund-raiser tonight, and one of my clients is sending someone to pick me up." He rubbed his neck. "I'm not looking forward to it, but I have to keep my clients happy."

"That's what I always say," Kate remarked blandly. She opened the passenger door of the Bug with a flourish. "Here you are."

Steven peered doubtfully inside.

"You've got to be kidding," he said.

Kate reached over and dumped all her rolls of wallpaper into the back seat, on top of the boxes of tiles. She couldn't see out the rear window anymore, but she was good at using her intuition.

"I'll take that flowerpot so you'll have a place to put your feet. All clear!"

Steven still looked doubtful, but he folded his rangy frame into the car beside Kate, his knees poking up at odd angles. She stared straight ahead, aware of how close she was to one of his broad shoulders. As she pulled out into traffic, a gauze scarf she'd misplaced drifted down from the piles in the back seat. It settled on Steven's shoulder like an indolent butterfly. Kate tried to pluck it away from him, but he got to it first. He weaved the golden cloth through his fingers.

"This reminds me of you," he murmured. "Bright and elusive. You're a mystery to me, Kate Melrose."

She didn't know how to answer that. He reached over and draped the scarf around her neck. His hands were so careful of her, withdrawing even as Kate wished for more of their touch. The scarf lay cool against the heated skin of her throat.

She was very glad to deliver Steven at his doorstep. He unfolded himself and climbed out of the car, while she sat for a minute trying to regain a professional demeanor. Fortunately all her workers had left right on schedule, so Steven would have the house to himself. But he seemed to be in a generous mood as he came around and leaned in her window.

"I'm going to help you unload your car before your shocks give out," he said. "And since I'll be gone tonight, I won't mind if you stay and wreak some havoc on the house."

"Why, thank you, Steven. Just wait—you're going to be pleased with the end result of all this, I promise." Now Kate felt a sense of camaraderie with Steven as the two of them lugged boxes into the storage room behind the kitchen. After that task was finished he went upstairs and Kate decided to tackle the awkward section of wallpapering in the hall. She'd chosen a pattern of violets and couldn't wait to see what it would look like.

The noise of the shower running carried down to her as she puttered about. It was far too intimate a sound, and Kate tried to blank it from her mind. She clambered up on the stepladder. The darn thing just wasn't tall enough; she had to stretch up on the very tips of her toes in order to reach any corners.

When Steven came downstairs, he was dressed in a tuxedo, which emphasized his dark hair, the clean lines of his features. The jacket was cut perfectly to the breadth of his shoulders. Kate found herself gaping at him. Before she knew it, she had teetered too far on the edge of the ladder. She came crashing down, helplessly raking her fingers against the plaster for a hold.

Steven was beside her in a second, kneeling down to extricate her from the rolls of wallpaper.

"Have you broken anything?" he demanded.

"No... Ouch!"

"What is it?"

"Another nail gone." She nursed the jagged edge of it, trying to scoot away from him. "Look out—you'll get all dirty."

"Don't be absurd." He took her elbow and managed to raise her to her feet. "Let me see your finger."

"It's just a nail, for goodness' sake!"

"Let me see it."

Unwillingly she gave him her hand. She stared at his immaculate white shirtfront and fought an overwhelming urge to nestle her dirt-smudged face against it. Her head moved imperceptibly yet dangerously closer to Steven's chest. He ran his fingers ever so gently over her cheek. It was just a breath of a touch, and yet it made her knees weaken.

"Kate..." he murmured. "Katherine?"

"No, actually it's Katarina." Her voice came shakily. "My mother is impossibly romantic. She didn't realize that I'm definitely a ... a Kate."

His chuckle was low and deep, sending a shivery warmth down her spine.

"And exactly what is the definition of a Kate?" he asked, his mouth close to her ear.

"Someone completely...completely sensible..." She closed her eyes, drawing in her breath as his rough-soft cheek moved against hers.

He held her for another moment, then released her slowly. "I'm sorry. I promised this wouldn't happen," he said. Kate trembled, feeling empty with Steven's arms no longer around her.

"Everything's fine," she declared, smoothing back her hair. "Just fine."

"I'm glad you're not angry."

"Why should I be angry?" she snapped.

Steven regarded her. "Because you're not the kind of woman who can be casual about a kiss," he said. "That's a refreshing quality. Don't try to hide it."

She lifted her chin. "I'm not trying to hide anything. It all seems very straightforward to me. We're business associates. We should avoid . . . certain things. But it's nothing—nothing to get worked up about." She folded her arms tightly, willing her heart to stop its tumult. Oh, she was angry all right—but mostly at herself. How could she respond so quickly to his touch?

The knocker at the front door rapped peremptorily, jarring Kate's taut nerves.

"That must be my ride," Steven said. "Be careful tonight. Don't kill yourself with that ladder."

"You don't need to worry about me. I'm perfectly capable of taking care of myself," she retorted. His expression was skeptical as he went to open the door.

A beautiful woman stood on the porch. No, she wasn't just beautiful; riveting was a more appropriate word to describe her. Luxuriant black hair flowed over her shoulders, and her mouth was an unabashed slash of scarlet in a cream-white face. Every curve of her stunning figure was tightly sheathed in green silk.

"My, my," the woman said, giving Steven a frank appraisal. "It looks like tonight is going to be promising, after all. I'm Gloria Nestor, Steve. Randolph sent me over to be your chauffeur for the night." She made "chauffeur" sound like something delightful and wicked, and her eyes roved over Steven as if he were a tall chocolate shake. Kate glanced at him to see how he was taking all this female admiration, but it was impossible to tell what he was thinking. Women probably looked at him like that all the time. Kate herself looked at him like that. It was a perfectly natural and perfectly annoying reaction!

"Gloria, I'd like you to meet Kate Melrose," Steven was saying, but Gloria barely flickered a glance in Kate's direction. She tucked her hand in the crook of Steven's arm, her jade-green fingernails resplendent against his tuxedo.

"Come on, Steve," she said in her throaty voice. "I'm going to show you what a warm and friendly place San Francisco can be."

Steven started to look over his shoulder at Kate, but Gloria Nestor proved she had muscle along with everything else as she squired Steven away.

Kate shut the door after them, leaning her forehead against it. The emptiness inside her was filling with a sharp pain whose source she didn't understand. It shouldn't bother her at all that Steven was spending the evening with a beautiful woman. He and Kate had agreed that their relationship ought to remain a strictly professional one—which didn't include any room for jealousy.

Kate hated herself for what she did next. She simply couldn't stop from running up to the landing window. She was just in time to see Gloria and Steven driving away in a sleek, dark green Jaguar. Kate's little yellow Bug looked dowdy and forlorn as the Jaguar swept past it.

Kate wilted and sank onto the stairway, rubbing her gold scarf against her cheek. But after a moment she sat up straight and glanced about defiantly in the gathering dusk. If she wanted, she could go out tonight herself. She pictured how she'd look, decked out in her corduroys and flowered shirt, her chipped nails displayed on Steven's tuxedoed arm. Then Gloria would appear, dazzling Steven in her designer gown—

This wasn't the right fantasy. Kate wrapped her arms around her knees and refocused her thoughts. She had that really fantastic evening dress she'd bought last year for the party with Myron. So what if Myron was just a family friend, a boy she'd grown up with and who was like one of her brothers. That didn't mean she couldn't toss on the dress at a moment's notice and go sailing off with some gorgeous male. Her brothers had plenty of friends she could rely on for the purpose!

Somehow the thought didn't cheer her up. Kate took a rag and started rubbing grime away from the newel post. But she couldn't concentrate on anything. All she could think about was Steven dancing close to Gloria in a ballroom somewhere. The thought was torment.

Kate threw down her rag. There was no peace here tonight. She had to get out. After all, she'd promised Paula that she would go over to Mrs. Cleeve's and discuss short tables. That was exactly what she'd do. Kate snatched up her briefcase and escaped.

CHAPTER FOUR

THE SUN WAS SHINING bright and clear the next morning as Kate wandered morosely along a downtown street. She should have been in the best of spirits, for all her favorite circumstances were combined here. It was Saturday, the best day of the week. She was out in the fresh air, treated to a spectacular view on all sides—delicate pagodas holding their ground against towering office buildings, the Bay Bridge rising in the distance. And she was surrounded by a myriad of enticing shop windows. Yes, the day should have been perfect, but all Kate could think about was Steven and Gloria Nestor. That was ruining everything.

It maddened Kate that she couldn't stop wondering how Steven had spent the evening. She longed to be as carefree, as independent of heart, as she'd always been before, no man disturbing her happiness. No unwanted emotions.

Kate trudged on aimlessly. But then a brass coat stand gleamed at her from one of the shop windows. It would be perfect for the entryway in Steven's house. Perfect . . . Kate walked into the store with a sense of purpose. She was beginning to feel a little better.

The coat stand was very expensive, but it was of excellent quality, the brass giving off a rich, mellow shine. And the house needed something exactly like this, even though it wasn't in Kate's original budget. She opened her checkbook to give its contents a hopeful perusal.

Her optimism was ill-founded. She had written quite a few checks lately for Steven's house, and had jotted the figures down hastily without subtracting them from her bank balance. Now she did some mental calculations, wincing at the results. She stuffed the checkbook back into her briefcase and fished for a credit card instead.

The sales clerk drifted away for a few minutes, then drifted back again.

"Denied," he said in a pale, expressionless voice.

Kate straightened up from her examination of an antique model ship. "Excuse me?" she said.

"Credit card denied."

"That's impossible!"

"Nothing's impossible."

"Good grief. Well...wait just a minute, please." She swung her briefcase up onto the counter and snapped it open in businesslike fashion. She started rummaging through her lipstick, lotion and spare packets of tissue. Oh, there was her travel sewing kit—the one she thought she'd lost.

The sales clerk leaned over the counter to observe. Kate drew her eyebrows together. Angling the briefcase smartly to block his view, she went on hunting. She pushed aside some spare change and a few tea bags. There it was—her other credit card, although this one looked a bit battered. She handed it crisply to the sales clerk.

This time she followed him. She hovered about as he passed her card through an obnoxious little machine.

"Also denied." The card came shooting back at her. She glanced suspiciously at the machine.

"There must be some mistake."

"No," the clerk said. He was beginning to look quite alert. "Want to try another one?"

"I think . . . I think that's enough, thank you." She turned and snapped her briefcase shut.

"You know what they say," he remarked in a dead-pan voice. "Third time lucky."

Kate felt totally flustered. She gazed at the coat stand. This was awful, just awful. She could have sworn she was nowhere near her credit limit.

The sales clerk was giving her a mild yet relentless stare. She retreated outside, and this time did not look in any shop windows as she hurried down the street. Steven's deposit money was gone, but she still had so much to do for the house. She'd already started the carpenters building more shelves, and they would be expecting payment soon. Things weren't going well with Mrs. Cleeve, either; last night's discussion about short tables had not been a success. Mrs. Cleeve had stared at Kate with a dour expression, like a latter-day Queen Victoria enthroned on cushions. Kate had tried refer-ring gently to Mrs. Cleeve's rheumatism, which acted up in San Francisco's damp climate; surely chairs and ordinary tables would be less of a strain. But Mrs. Cleeve had remained adamant about her Japanese mo-tif, and Kate had gone home with a leg cramp from sit-ting on a pillow.

Now she headed for her car. Everything was getting out of hand, yet the only solution she could think of at the moment was to retreat to McClary Hill. She'd have the house to herself and perhaps the solitude would in-spire her. When she arrived, however, she found that Steven's Mercedes was back from the shop and parked in the driveway. Kate pulled up beside it, grateful not to see any dark green Jaguars.

She'd been able to make at least one purchase this morning—two cans of paint stripper. She began lugging them toward the porch. A bee buzzed lazily past her into the garden, distracting her for a moment. Weeds had taken over all the flower beds; only a few hardy rosebushes still flourished, growing wild now. The stone fountain was mournfully dry, with a stone sailing ship beached on a pedestal in its center. She'd have to do something about all this neglect. Everywhere she turned, another part of the house begged for her attention. Somehow she had to find enough money to provide the right care.

Kate's arms were aching as she toiled up the steps of the porch. The front door swung open in front of her, and there was Steven. Her eyes began at the toes of his running shoes, traveled up the lean length of his jean-clad legs, stopped at the faded blue cotton that strained across his shoulders.

"On your way out?" she said hopefully to his chest as she backed away.

"As a matter of fact, no." He took the heavy cans from her and set them inside the door.

"Mrs. Adler said you'd be working in your office all weekend."

"I changed my mind."

"I see." Kate straightened a crease on her canvas pants. "Well...I hope you had a good time last night at your fund-raiser," she said insincerely.

"It was fair," he said. "Nothing special. I had Gloria drop me back here early so I could study some contracts."

"I see." Good grief, Kate berated herself, couldn't she think of anything else to say? But her heart was lightened with the knowledge that Gloria had not completely dazzled Steven. She found herself grinning foolishly at him.

"Where are those shutters that needed hanging?" he asked.

"What?"

"Shutters. Those things you hang outside windows—"

"You're not supposed to do any work on the house," Kate protested.

"It's my house. If I want to hang shutters, that's what I'll do."

"I didn't mean it that way," she said, poking her sneaker at a pile of old boards. "I mean—if you *want* to work on the house, fine. But you don't have to. I take full responsibility for the job I set out for myself—"

"Kate," Steven said with a sigh, "where are the shutters?"

An hour or so later Kate sat back from stripping the wainscoting in the library, glad to see that she was right about it. The natural grain was going to look beautiful in here. She stood up and stretched, gratified at how easy it was to work with Steven close by. She went over to the window, listening to the cheerful sound of nails being hammered into wood. Equally cheery was the sound of whistling. Goodness, the man whistled Mozart? Kate smiled; her financial problems were beginning to fade into the background. She resumed stripping paint.

She was deeply engrossed when Steven poked his head inside the room. "Lunch is served," he announced. "Meet me in the kitchen in five minutes." He disappeared before she could say anything. Mystified, she cleaned up in the washroom and then went to see what he was concocting.

It turned out to be a giant, impressive-looking omelet. Kate breathed in the aroma of onions and chives.

"I didn't know you could cook," she said, taking two plates from the cupboard. "That smells wonderful."

"I have a few surprises up my sleeve," he said.

"Oh, I'll vouch for that," she returned, opening the drawer where the plastic forks and spoons were kept. Here was another surprise already—the plastic had been replaced by a set of stainless steel. Kate picked up a spoon and examined it critically. Nothing fancy, but certainly serviceable. She nodded, only to glance over and find Steven watching her sardonically.

"Well, I'm glad you're finally settling in," she told him.

"You didn't even notice the new drain board. You're slipping, Ms Melrose."

"It's a wonderful tray," she pronounced. "But didn't they have it in any color besides olive green?"

"Will you stop trying to color-coordinate my life?" he grumbled.

"No," Kate said happily. The best surprise of all today was how comfortable she felt with Steven. She sat down with him and they shared their meal in companionable silence. The omelet was delicious.

"Did your mother teach you to cook like that?" Kate asked, leaning back luxuriously.

"No, actually it was my father. My mother's idea of cooking is peanut-butter-and-jelly sandwiches."

"She sounds interesting." Kate propped her elbows on the table, while Steven regarded his plate thoughtfully.

"I suppose she is," he finally replied. "She's always curious about life, always reaching out for more of it. She was the one who'd go out sledding with us, while my father had his head in a book—the perfect university professor." Steven spoke softly, musingly. "My mother couldn't stand to be cooped up like that. She'd been a professional skier, and the career that really made her happy was giving skiing lessons." He chuckled. "She'd have all us kids lined up on the slopes with her other students. She didn't care how many times we fell down."

Kate was listening intently. "That sounds so exotic to me. All that snow, and skiing from the time you're a kid. I never learned at all."

"It's not too late. You could start now."

Kate shivered, just thinking about the cold and the snow and ice. "Actually, I'd do really well in the lodge—with one of those big fuzzy sweaters and a cup of hot chocolate."

"I'd get you out on the slopes first thing," Steven said. "You'd like it."

"No, I wouldn't," Kate said stubbornly. "I like driving down hills, not skiing down them."

"How do you know if you've never tried it?" he asked.

"I just know, that's all. It's not my idea of fun. What's wrong with that?"

Now he was leaning toward her. "You're being narrow-minded. That really surprises me."

She glared at him. "Maybe it's just too much for you—a woman having her own interests. Maybe you just want a clone of yourself, up there on the slopes with you."

"How the hell did you jump to a conclusion like that?" He glared back at her. "All right, so I think people should be willing to try new things."

"What if I tried it?" she asked guardedly. "What if I tried skiing and decided I didn't like it? What would you say then?"

"I'd say you didn't give it enough of a chance."

Her fork clattered down on her plate. "Talk about narrow-minded," she said in disgust. "You think a woman should want to do everything *you* do."

"Listen, I grew up and saw my parents not have a thing in common. Two people need to share interests."

"As long as they're the man's, right?" she taunted him.

"Dammit, I never said that."

"You didn't have to. But I think your parents sound charming. A skier and a professor. Variety is what makes life interesting." She gathered up the plates with a great deal more clatter. "Gloria Nestor probably skis," she muttered, but was instantly sorry she had spoken the words out loud.

"I'll ask her when I see her tonight," Steven said.

"Fine." Kate stood at the counter, battling a wretched wave of jealousy.

"She'll be at my client's for dinner. He does a lot of business with her."

"It's no concern of mine how or when you see Gloria Nestor," Kate said stiffly. "I don't know why you feel the need to explain anything to me."

"I don't know why, either," Steven said, "but there it is."

Kate swiped at crumbs on the counter with a paper towel. A wayward image crept into her mind: she and

Steven bundled up in mittens and mufflers, out on a snowy mountaintop together . . . just the two of them.

That was the frightening thing. Even though she *knew* she'd hate skiing, part of her longed to go out there and make herself cold and miserable. Just so she could be on that mountaintop with Steven. Just so she could be his type of woman over all the Gloria Nestors of the world. And there would go her selfhood, the independent person she'd fought so hard to become. Yes, it was frightening, wanting so badly to please a man.

She pushed the plates across the counter. She wasn't going anywhere near that sink today. It was far too dangerous.

"I'll get back to work," she said briskly. "Thanks for the lunch."

"You're welcome." But his tone didn't sound welcome in the least. When he went back outside, the pounding of nails sounded a bit more vigorous than necessary. The whistling had stopped.

Kate paced the library floor. She took a bag of M&Ms from her pocket and lined them all up in a straight row on the mantel. She picked out the yellow ones and ate them. Gloria Nestor had wasted no time in arranging another evening with Steven, and perhaps this time she'd be more successful in keeping his interest.

"She can have him!" Kate declared to the mantelpiece, but the words didn't sound very convincing. She ate one green M&M, then stalked upstairs to look for anything that would make her stop brooding about Steven and Gloria.

She paused in a doorway, examining the ratty brown carpet she'd started to pull up. This was the room where she planned to hang Steven's print once it was framed.

Whenever she saw a painting by Monet she would think of Steven.

This wasn't doing her any good. Turning, Kate opened the door across the hall. She saw a pair of loafers discarded carelessly on the rag rug, a shirt tossed across the back of a chair. Steven's bedroom. Kate hesitated, then stepped inside. There was only the barest amount of furniture—a couple of chairs, a bed, a nightstand. Kate picked up the book that was open facedown on the nightstand and read the title: *The Hound of the Baskervilles*. Sherlock Holmes—that seemed right for Steven. She glanced down, eyes lingering on the rumpled sheets of his bed. His pillow had been twisted and punched up against the wall as if he, too, had spent a restless night. Kate moved her hand over the pillow, thinking of his tousled head pressed against it. She could so easily imagine his powerful body lying here, tensed with energy even in sleep. Her hand crept downward, fingering a corner of the sheet....

What had come over her? She straightened quickly and backed away. She turned and fled the room, retreating all the way to the attic.

Here at last she found something to occupy her mind. She began poking about among all the boxes. This mess really did need to be cleared out, and yet the place would lose much of its atmosphere all neat and bare. Attics were meant for treasures like this.

She found fifty-year-old receipts, mildewed books, a moth-eaten scarf, faded photographs of children playing on a beach. Kate settled down cross-legged on the floor, sneezed vigorously into her handkerchief, and proceeded to pore over the photographs. Young faces laughed up at her, their happiness shining even through the cracked, yellowed film of age. Kate wondered if the children had grown up in this house, where they were now. All the papers she had unearthed so far carried the name Eliza R. Hobbes. Who was she? Had she loved the house as much as Kate did?

Reluctantly she put the photos back in their shoe box, but couldn't resist scavenging through a big chest pushed against one wall. It was filled with old dresses, the cloth thin and brittle under Kate's fingers.

"Oh, goodness," she breathed, holding up a whirl of polka dots, then a froth of yellowed lace. Perhaps Eliza had worn these dresses to boating parties, or leisurely lunches in someone's garden. But here was a gown that surely had been worn to a ball. It was simple yet strikingly elegant, an off-the-shoulder burgundy silk with a full skirt swirling to the floor. Kate held it gently against her body, closing her eyes and humming a waltz to herself. She could see a string orchestra playing in a ballroom where couples skimmed over the parquet floors. Unbidden, an image of Steven rose to her mind, the way he had looked last night in his tuxedo. He fit too easily into her fantasy; it was too easy to imagine him clasping her hand in his and leading her out onto the dance floor. He pulled her close, his cheek resting against her hair.

Kate hummed her waltz louder, with a deliberately martial beat, but that didn't stop the Steven in her dream from drawing her a little closer.

"You look beautiful," he said huskily. Kate froze and her eyes flew open. Steven was sitting next to the trap door, gazing at her intently. The blood rushed to her face, and she lost her grip on the dress. It floated down to the dusty floorboards. She grappled for it, but in one easy motion Steven stood and was beside her. He rescued the dress, brushing it off and handing it back to her. The ceiling was so low that he had to lean over her. Kate took a deep, shuddering breath, and the next second she was in Steven's arms, the dress crushed against her.

"Please, please, no..." she whispered, but her words were lost as his mouth descended hungrily to hers. No fantasy could have captured the actual feel of him—the searing pressure of his lips, the lean hard strength of his body. Fire coursed through her in response, sweeping away all her defenses. Her hands moved upward over his shoulders. His muscles tightened under her touch, and he gave a low groan. The silk rustled between them, unheeded.

Her body fit so closely against his, but she longed to be closer yet. The need in her was overwhelming, more terrifying than any sensation she had ever known. She felt powerless against it. Her lips opened willingly to the gentle but insistent probing of his tongue. He tasted fresh and warm and clean.

But then he broke away from her, and the attic suddenly seemed cold, despite its stuffy air. They were both breathing raggedly. Kate held the gown against her as if for protection.

"Lord...that shouldn't have happened," Steven said.

"No," she agreed woodenly, not understanding how fire could bank down so suddenly to ashes.

"You'll have to forgive me—and forget about it."

But it was already too late. She knew that her body would always remember the feel and taste of him.

"I suppose that will be easy for you," she burst out. "To forget you came up here and—"

"Nothing is easy with you, Kate," he said roughly. His eyes were darkened now with some emotion she could not fathom. She turned away, clutching the dress still tighter.

"You're the one making everything so difficult," she muttered. "You weren't even supposed to be here today."

"You're right. I don't know what the hell I'm doing here. I've got a pile of contracts waiting for me at the office. That's where I should have been in the first place." He left her abruptly.

Kate felt raw inside. Slowly she loosened her grip on the poor gown, making a futile attempt to smooth out the wrinkles. It still felt warm from the contact with Steven. She returned it to the old chest, then sank down and rested her forehead against her knees. She was completely drained and completely shaken. How foolish it was to daydream, to imagine a perfect romantic scene. Because the reality was far too dangerous, pushing her to acknowledge feelings better left ignored.

But she could not deny the sensations that Steven aroused in her. They were not merely physical. She could have dealt with that—explained them away as the normal responses of a healthy body. But what Steven made her feel . . .

She straightened, rubbing her temples. This feeling went too deep, touching some place inside her that she'd never known existed before. And then to suffer the coldness, the hurt when he withdrew his arms, to wonder about the woman he'd be seeing tonight . . .

She scrambled to her feet. Things had gone too far, but it still wasn't too late to save herself, to keep herself emotionally intact. She was convinced of that. She'd always been in control of her own life, and that wasn't about to change. She wouldn't let it. Kate slammed down the lid of the chest, but then lifted it up again to tuck in a wayward corner of the burgundy gown. The poor thing shouldn't suffer just because of Steven Reid.

Later that afternoon Kate paid an unexpected visit to her mother, and that alone was a measure of how badly she'd been shaken. It was never easy to return to the house she'd grown up in, to reenter a world she had escaped at eighteen. She went there now without quite knowing what she expected to gain, just knowing that she had to go.

She drove slowly, however, wanting to prolong her enjoyment of the beauty around her. For Kate, San Francisco had always been a city of color. It wasn't just the vivid blue of the sky and the bay. It was the exuberance of all those Victorian houses, flaunting their bright new coats of paint: green, red, purple, orange, yellow. Gables, columns and trim had colors all their own, decorating the houses like extra swirls of frosting on a cake.

But there was at least one street in town where no one had caught the spirit of color. Kate turned onto it and pulled up in front of one of the small, dreary houses. Here and there an individual touch defied the uniform drabness of the street: a scraggly bush trimmed into pompons, a window box of geraniums, a door painted apple green. But the house where Kate's mother still lived exhibited no such rebellion. The outside walls were a dingy and faded tan. How Kate had always hated them! With a sigh she climbed out of the Bug. She brought along the silk roses she'd managed to buy after dipping into just a bit of her rent money. She could never come here without a gift of something beautiful.

The door flew open at her knock, and she was swept up into a flurry of kittens, fuzzy slippers and billows of material in an alarming pattern of muddy red poppies. Her mother's arms embraced her, silk flowers and all.

"Oh, they're lovely, Katie. You always bring me the loveliest things. I'm so happy to see you, dear. Come along!" Lorna Melrose sped down the hall, her slippers moving at a good clip. One kitten was hooked under her arm, two others scurried at her heels. How many more might be hiding in the poppy housecoat that enveloped Lorna's plump figure? Kate smiled, remembering how as a child she had cried into and been comforted by her mother's too-big housecoats. Mrs. Melrose had never complained when her children clutched at her with sticky hands and teary faces. She was the same way with her many grandchildren now. Kate might have wished to change a lot of things about her mother, but never, never those all-comforting housecoats.

"I know just the thing for these roses. Yes, yes, let me see..." Lorna popped into a closet overflowing with clothes, an old badminton set and several umbrellas. "Dear me, help me out, Katie." Kate found herself balancing two kittens in her arms, as well as the flowers. A moment later her mother emerged triumphantly clutching a box overflowing with tissue paper. Her cheeks were pink under the flyaway gray hair. "The cut-glass vase you gave me. It'll be perfect."

"Oh, Mother!" Kate exclaimed, a kitten ear tickling her nose. "Do you mean it's been in the box all this time? I gave it to you so you could enjoy it."

"But I *have* enjoyed it, dear. Knowing it's safe here, in all its loveliness. And now you've brought roses that will always be in bloom. I knew I was saving this for just the right moment. Go ahead, dear, arrange the flowers.

I've always loved to watch you with them, from the time you were a little girl."

Kate managed to deposit the kittens on the floor. She began filling the vase, automatically placing the flowers to the best effect. She had never been able to explain to her mother that beauty was not something to be hoarded. It was to be savored every moment, until your whole life was filled with it. If a vase broke, then you bought another one that was even prettier.

"Why, that's lovely, Katie. Just lovely. You have the touch." Lorna Melrose plunked two cups of peppermint tea down on the torn oilcloth that covered the table. "Sit down, sit down. You're always in such a rush. That's better." She bustled around the table. "Do you remember how you loved the flower vendors as a child? We used to walk along the street, and I'd tell you stories about the roses and mums and gladiolas."

Kate grinned. "The one I liked the best was about the white rose, and all the quests it went on trying to find colors so that it would be as beautiful as the red rose. Oh, Mother, you tell the most wonderful stories! When are you going to start writing some of them down?"

"I'm thinking about it, I really am. All the pictures in my mind, years and years of them. I've just never had the time to put them down on paper." Lorna sent the cracked sugar bowl sailing down the table toward her daughter. "What a life we had, your father and I! But we pulled through it together, didn't we?"

Kate didn't answer. She took a spoonful of sugar and dumped it into her cup. Her father had been a dour man, difficult to please. But her mother had never stopped trying, fluttering around him anxiously and beaming whenever he actually nodded his approval.

"What about that easel I bought for you?" Kate said at last. "You have the time now for your pictures and stories."

"With your sister Justine and the three children coming for dinner tonight? I haven't any time at all! But why don't you join us, Katie?"

"Maybe another time. Just do some sketches, why don't you? Just something to get started."

"Of course, dear. You know I've always wanted to paint. It was my big dream."

"Yes," Kate said softly. "That's what you always told me." She stood up and moved restlessly around the room. Her father had never wanted his wife to study art. He'd said it was a waste of time. He had said the same thing to Kate when she announced her dream of art school. Unlike her mother, she hadn't listened. She had defied him and followed her dream.

Now she frowned at the spot on the wall where her brother Benjamin had tried to glue a chair when he was nine.

"Mother, why don't you let me redo this house for you? It could be absolutely stunning. This place has good lines."

"And wouldn't I be proud! My house decorated by the best designer in California. Yes, dear, someday when we both have the time." Lorna settled into a chair for a moment, two kittens attacking each other in her lap. Kate eyed the one with black boots and a black tail.

"Aren't there more of them than the last time I was here?" she murmured.

"Goodness, do you really think so?" Lorna peered down at the floor and wiggled her slippers. They were pounced on by a tiger-striped kitten.

Kate took another turn around the room. These days she felt an overpowering restlessness whether she sat or stood.

"What's the matter, Katie?" Mrs. Melrose prodded. "You're different somehow today. Is it a man?"

"Good grief, Mother! Why on earth would you say something like that?"

"Lucky guess. What's his name?"

"That's ridiculous. There *is* no man," Kate lied desperately.

"Someday you'll understand, my dear. A woman just isn't complete without that one certain man."

"Mother!"

"Just as a man isn't complete until he finds the woman meant for *him*. Look at your father and me. He may be gone, the dear man, but what we had is still here. It's still alive in all of us."

Kate stopped pacing. She clenched her hands, wanting to protest. But she had long since learned that her mother would never, ever allow anyone to speak against her husband. His memory was sacred.

Kate went over and kissed Lorna's cheek. The skin was still fresh and youthful under the untidy gray hair, and smelled comfortingly of primrose soap.

"I really must run, Mother. Say hello to Justine and the kids for me."

"Very well, but come back soon, Katie. You know I always love to see you. And bring your young man along."

"Mother, there *is* no young man!"

"Whatever you say, dear, but I'd still like to meet him."

Kate left the house, shaking her head. At least now she knew why she'd come here today. It wasn't just for maternal comfort. She'd needed to remind herself what could happen when a woman gave up her independence for a man. Her mother had given up everything from the very beginning, just for the chance of winning and keeping one man. Kate couldn't allow that to happen to herself. She'd fought too hard to escape her parents' home and what it meant. She wouldn't let any man take charge of her happiness, her life. Especially not Steven Reid.

"That's right, Steven," she declared, climbing back into her Bug and accelerating forcefully. "Especially not you."

CHAPTER FIVE

KATE TRIED TO BE CASUAL, flipping through magazines in the reception area of Steven's office. She'd spent the rest of the weekend searching for a way out of her financial bind, only to return again and again to the same inevitable solution. This time she had been the one to arrange an appointment with Steven.

Now Mrs. Adler looked up from her typewriter to give an encouraging smile. Kate wondered if the businesslike secretary gave that smile to everyone who waited out here, or merely to those who seemed most in need of fortitude. The prospect of venturing into Steven's office was certainly daunting.

Kate set the magazine down, crossed her legs and then uncrossed them. Her dress of turquoise blue settled in soft folds about her, the color giving her confidence. She glanced around. The walls were painted stark white—of course—and the carpet was a dull gray. Only a few pictures adorned the room: nondescript scenes in muted shades. Even Mrs. Adler was dressed in a subdued gray suit, her brown hair drawn tightly back. Kate shifted in her hard, straight-backed chair, only to receive another smile from Mrs. Adler. Goodness, this was worse than waiting to see the dentist.

Mrs. Adler's telephone buzzed once and she answered it instantly. "Yes, Mr. Reid?... Of course, Mr. Reid." She replaced the receiver gingerly, then slid out of her chair. "Mr. Reid will see you now," she said in a hushed tone. She tiptoed down the hall, leading Kate to the inner sanctum.

Kate lifted her head and sailed into the office straight past Mrs. Adler's horrified gaze.

"Good morning, Steven," she said cheerily. "Wonderful weather, don't you think? Of course, you can't see a bit of it in this gloom. There...that's better." Kate yanked on the blinds, sending a dazzle of sunlight into the room. Mrs. Adler choked.

"Oh, Mr. Reid..." she sputtered.

"It's perfectly all right, Mrs. Adler," Steven said dryly. "Ms Melrose has a way of taking over a room."

His secretary hesitated but finally retreated, the door closing slowly behind her.

Steven was standing with his elbows propped on the back of a big, ugly leather chair. But that didn't stop him from looking fresh and vibrant, as if he'd carried a brisk ocean breeze right into this dreary office. Kate imagined him at the helm of an old sailing ship, a rakish sea captain...

Why did he have to affect her like this? She sank down in the chair across from his desk, her dress floating about her. Steven's eyes swept over her as he moved around his big, unwieldy chair and settled into it. They had not seen each other since their kiss in the attic, but Kate's heart still felt bruised. He had rejected her that day; perhaps only a glamorous and sophisticated woman like Gloria Nestor could touch his heart. Kate sat up a little straighter, reminding herself fiercely that emotional independence was the most important thing in the world to her. She had to hold on to it.

"What can I do for you?" Steven asked curtly. She struggled to gaze back at him with equanimity.

"You really ought to do something about this place. It has no flair at all."

The barest trace of a smile crossed his mouth. "Did you actually come here to redecorate my office?"

"I wanted to talk to you about your house. It's really coming along well, isn't it?" she asked brightly. He drummed his fingers on the large, featureless desk. He looked powerful and dynamic, his hair springing back from his forehead in the way she found so appealing.

"Every wall half-painted," he said. "Stacks of tiles in my bathtub. Curtains all over the chairs but none on the windows. You haven't finished one single room!"

"I'm glad you brought up that point, Steven. You see, I work with an overall scheme in mind. It's very important to stay in keeping with the entire spirit of the house."

"The place isn't haunted. You don't have to pacify any ghosts."

"Well, the house does have a history. We can't ignore that."

"Of course not," he muttered. "We wouldn't want to just paint the damn thing and be done with it."

She smiled at him but he didn't smile back.

"Kate, I assume there's a point to all this."

She sighed. Steven wasn't making things easy for her. It wasn't as though she'd *wanted* to come here today. She didn't have any other choice, that was all. Poking through her briefcase, she extracted a slightly wrinkled sheet of paper. She pushed it across the desk toward him.

"There. I wanted you to see exactly what I've spent so far. I wanted you to have the whole picture."

He scowled down at the sheet of paper.

"Are you serious? It takes that many cans of paint to come up with 'persimmon pink'? I hate pink."

"I'm using it very judiciously—as an accent color."

"Why the hell did you buy me a wok? And I don't need a chandelier."

"Yes, you do. It's going to look wonderful in the dining room, all those prisms of glass capturing the light! I can hardly wait until it's up."

Steven did not seem to share her enthusiasm. "What's this about more carpentry work?" he demanded. "You told me you were only going to have a few repairs done."

"I know you'll be happy with all the extra shelf space that's being put in. And I think one of the carpenters has a crush on Paula. His name is Jerry and he's very enterprising." Kate saw from the expression on Steven's face that this information wasn't going over too well. In fact, the entire discussion wasn't proceeding as planned. She had wanted to prove to Steven that she knew exactly where his money had gone, and that each expenditure was completely justified. But somehow she didn't seem to be getting this across to him. She decided to plunge right ahead.

"You see, Steven, the house has required a greater initial outlay than I anticipated. I'll therefore have to request . . . an additional amount of money from you." She pushed another sheet of paper toward him, this one smudged from a great deal of figuring, erasing and more figuring. "You can see it all right here. I'll need to purchase more furnishings, of course, and settle up with the carpenters. By the way, I'm sure you'll agree that I'm being very reasonable about the fee for all my extra time." She felt triumphant now that the words were out, but Steven's expression still wasn't encouraging.

"You signed an agreement with me, Kate. I'm not obligated to hand over one more cent to you until the job is finished."

"Things have evolved since then!" she protested.

"Is this how you usually operate your business?" he asked in a quiet but steely tone. "You renege on agreements and buy woks for people who don't want them?"

"Your house is a special case," she returned. "I've never encountered such neglect before. Besides, you have to see the difference between the letter of the law and the spirit of it—"

"Spirits again! Let's stick with facts here," he interrupted. "For one thing, who does your books?"

"I handle my own accounting," she said. "With Paula's help, of course. She's very good with numbers."

Steven rubbed his jaw. "What was your net profit last year?"

"Well, um—" Kate shifted in her chair "—it wasn't bad."

"You're not really sure, are you? You probably took a loss."

"Not much of one," she said defensively. She was beginning to feel as though she were on the witness stand.

"What kind of advertising campaign do you have?" he went on in that calm, relentless tone.

"We're in the yellow pages," she said proudly. "Melrose Designs. You can look it up right now."

"Do you know what deductions to make on your tax return? Do you depreciate your business equipment?

Have you established a good, solid relationship with your banker? Good Lord, do you even *have* a banker?''

Kate felt like a criminal under cross-examination. ''I plead the Fifth,'' she muttered. Steven raised an eyebrow.

''It's worse than I thought,'' he remarked. ''You run your business like a one-woman demolition derby. For your own good I'm not going to give you any more money.''

Kate was not defeated. She stood up so that she could give Steven her most forceful glare. For added emphasis she leaned across his desk.

''We're talking about your house, Steven. Your home! It could be a *real* home if you'd just let me do my job. The kind of place that has a stack of firewood by the hearth and wind chimes outside the window.'' Kate's cheeks were flushed, the blood pumping through her body. She forgot all the arguments she'd rehearsed in front of her mirror, and the words just tumbled out of her. She looked straight into Steven's eyes.

''I know what you want deep down, Steven—a place to remind you of that drafty old house in Vermont where you grew up. But you want a place that's different, too, your own personal idea of what a home should be. The first time you saw the house on McClary Hill, you recognized what you'd been looking for. You didn't even know you'd been looking, but then you saw it, the home that *could* be. I see it, too. That's why you can't turn me down, Steven. It's your vision of the house I'm bringing to life!''

She stopped, out of breath and rather alarmed by what she'd said. She hadn't realized any of this before today, but every instinct told her it was the truth: she and Steven shared the same dream of what a home should be. The dream bound them together with its power, perhaps irrevocably. Kate's arms were trembling as she pressed her hands against Steven's desk. He gazed at her seriously, all mockery gone.

Neither one of them said anything for a long moment. Then Steven brought out a checkbook and started writing in it, his pen scratching over the paper. Kate straightened, drained by the encounter. Steven tore off the check and handed it to her.

"Thank you," she said formally, depositing it in her briefcase.

"None of this changes my mind, Kate. You've still gone too far with my house. Way too far. And you definitely need help managing your business."

"I'm happy with things just the way they are," she declared.

"A manager would help you channel your money and time. You'd be more productive."

"I'm already productive. And right now I don't have to answer to anyone else. I'm going to keep it that way."

"You're making a mistake."

She ignored his warning, glancing around at his bare walls and ugly furniture. "You really should let me do something about your office."

"I'll think about it," he said agreeably. "Maybe we should do the place in persimmon pink."

She frowned at him. He looked far too attractive with his devilish grin.

"Goodbye, Steven. Thank you. I mean—goodbye." She swept out of the room and past the disapproving gaze of Mrs. Adler. She didn't need anyone telling her how to manage her business. Everything was under control: the carpenters would get their money, Paula and Max would have a few weeks' salary, and Kate could pay her electric bill.

Most important of all, she could continue furnishing Steven's house like a real home. Over the next few days she lavished her love on the old place, bringing all sorts of gifts to it—an antique rolltop desk, a china butter dish, two large bath towels decorated with black Scotties in red bows. It was like celebrating the home's long-forgotten birthdays.

By the time Saturday came around again, Kate had also purchased the tools she needed to make her advance into the garden. She spent a contented morning raking up ancient leaves and poking into hardened earth with a spade. Then she crawled under the hedge, humming to herself and enjoying the good, clean snap of shears on dead branches.

Kate heard the sound of a car driving up, and a moment later an elegant pair of high-heeled shoes strolled into her line of vision. The shoes were glossy black patent leather, cut in simple lines to display a graceful set of ankles. Kate inched herself out from under the hedge and stood up. Gloria Nestor faced her, looking polished in a mint-green linen suit and a black silk blouse. Kate glanced down at her own T-shirt with its ripped hem and her denim shorts, which had been patched in three different places. Just being around Gloria made her feel inadequate. Gloria's assurance was obviously more than skin-deep; she carried herself like a woman who had believed in herself since babyhood. But she was not dismissive today, and she greeted Kate pleasantly.

"Hello," she said. "I was looking for Steve, but I suppose he isn't home."

"No, he's not," Kate answered.

"That's too bad. I wanted to ask him to pick me up early before the opera tonight."

It hurt to know that Steven was going out with Gloria; it hurt far too much. "I'm sure you can call him later," Kate said mechanically.

"Yes, I'll do that," Gloria said, but she made no move to leave. Instead she perched herself on the edge of the stone fountain, her beautiful ankles crossed casually in front of her. "Steve was telling me how you're transforming his house," she went on. "He says you're quite a talented decorator."

Kate was skeptical about that last comment. The Steven *she* knew was less than flattering about what she'd been doing to his house. She smiled a little to herself.

"I'm sure that it's a very gratifying experience, working with Steve," Gloria said. "Just between us girls, Kate, he's quite an unusual man."

"Yes, well, I suppose he is," Kate answered cautiously. She wasn't sure where this conversation was headed.

"It's not just that he's so attractive, although that certainly counts for a lot," Gloria elaborated. "He's intelligent, sensitive and caring. He's also potentially one of the most successful lawyers in the country."

Kate picked a twig out of her hair. Yes, Steven Reid was all those things, as well as stubborn, impatient and opinionated. He wouldn't be nearly as interesting a person without such traits. Gloria made him sound like a saint. How dull that would be!

Gloria was observing her too carefully, Kate thought, annoyed by the undercurrents she sensed.

"How much of your message do you actually want me to relay to Steven?" she asked without ceremony.

"Oh, Steve already knows what a high regard I have for him," Gloria said easily. "I was just wondering how you felt about him, Kate, and it's clear that you share my opinion."

Kate said nothing to this, sure that Gloria would use any information she gleaned today to suit her own purposes. At last Gloria stood up, shaking back her lustrous mane of hair. Her eyes were oddly opaque, so dark they were almost black, and they were impossible to read.

"I've enjoyed chatting with you, Kate," she said, sounding companionable and completely sincere. "I'd like to talk to you again sometime. I might be able to throw some decorating business your way."

"I have more than I can handle right now," Kate said.

"You should always cultivate your contacts," Gloria answered coolly. "I could be of invaluable assistance to you in your career. Goodbye now. Please do tell Steve that I stopped by to see him."

Kate nodded grudgingly, still feeling at a disadvantage. She watched as the dark green Jaguar purred out the drive and down McClary Hill.

Gloria Nestor was an enigma. She had seemed genuinely pleased to talk to Kate and hadn't sounded patronizing even when she gave the advice about cultivating contacts. And yet something rang false; Gloria seemed to have an ulterior motive in coming here today. She probably hadn't even intended to see Steven at all. More than likely she'd come to check out the competition—Kate.

Kate poked her fingers into her new pair of flowered gardening gloves. Competing with Gloria for Steven's affections seemed so foolish, so hazardous. Already she was too bound to Steven, wondering if she would ever be able to break completely free of him. Already she felt too much pain just knowing that Steven and Gloria would spend another evening together.

Kate pulled off her gloves and tossed them down like gauntlets, in a challenge to herself. She wouldn't succumb to the hurt inside her, but would battle it with wholesome physical labor. She strode over to the new lawn mower she'd purchased, pushing it around to the back of the house where the lawn sloped down before her in a wild tangle of grass. She yanked on the starter and the machine leapt into life, traveling forward with a momentum all its own. Kate pulled on the handle, but it was already too late. The lawn mower had gained speed and was racing down the steep hill. All she could do was hang on and fly along after it.

They both landed in a clump of quack grass, and the engine cut off abruptly. Kate struggled to her feet, brushing off her shorts and craning her neck to stare up at the house. The steepness of the lawn was more than she'd bargained for, but she wasn't defeated yet. She grasped the handle of the mower and started pulling it back up the hill. Every muscle straining against the force of gravity, she advanced a little—then a little more.

"What's going on now?" Steven's voice demanded from above her. She stopped, the sweat trickling down her face. She didn't dare look up for fear of losing her grip.

"Hello, Steven. I'm mowing, as you can see."

"I can see, all right."

"Well . . . so, if you don't mind, I'll just get on with it." She licked the corner of her mouth. Her hands were beginning to slip from perspiration and she bent back a little further against the weight of the machine.

"You're supposed to be an interior decorator," Steven's voice shot down to her. "Not an exterior one!"

"Well, you know what we were talking about the other day," she panted. "My overall scheme? If I'm going to look at the house—as a whole—I have to include the lawn—" The mower slipped out of her grasp and went crashing down the hill. She tried to look as if that was exactly what she'd intended. Taking out her bandanna—*his* bandanna—she patted her face.

Steven climbed down beside her. He seemed ready for a good argument, but then he simply looked at her. His gaze felt like a caress.

"Sunlight," he said musingly. "You have eyes full of sunlight. Did you know that?"

Kate stared at the soft cotton of his shirt. She stood without moving, almost without breathing. She knew she should turn away from him before her defenses crumbled, yet everything in her ached to be near him.

"Gloria came by," she blurted out, using the words as a barrier. "She wanted you to pick her up early tonight . . . before the opera."

Steven looked puzzled. "What opera? Nobody told me about this."

"Gloria didn't say anything else about it."

Steven groaned. "My client keeps arranging these evenings of his without consulting me first. I hate opera."

Kate rubbed a scrape on her elbow. She had assumed that Steven and Gloria would be sharing an intimate evening alone. But apparently it wasn't going to be like that at all! Kate felt a surge of relief and happiness. The intensity of her emotions startled her, but anything to do with Steven seemed to affect her this way—no half-measures allowed. He reached out a hand and gently cupped her chin. Now a sensual lassitude took her over, as if his touch could still all her fears of him. Her lips parted and her breath came on a slow, deep sigh.

"We seem to have a problem," she managed to say. "This physical attraction—both of us..."

"We ought to be able to work it out," Steven said. "We're two adults."

"Two responsible adults," she agreed. She curled her fingers to keep them from reaching out to him.

"So we won't take this any further," he said.

"We did agree to be professional..." She raised her eyes slowly to his.

"Dammit, Kate!" He bent his head and kissed her, his lips firm and demanding. She returned the kiss steadily, making her own demands.

Then it was over. Steven lifted his head and stepped back from her.

"There," he said.

She widened her eyes. "Well. Now *that's* out of the way—" she began.

"Don't you feel better?"

She wouldn't admit it, but she did feel better. This time there was no sense of horrible rejection, no coldness afterward. It had been a most satisfying kiss, exquisitely complete in itself. How could Steven's lips tutor her in so many different emotions?

She made herself speak in a calm, analytical manner. "We're going to ruin our business relationship," she said. "If we keep on this way, we won't be able to avoid it."

"We can't deny the attraction between us," Steven answered, sounding equally reasonable. "That's what we've been trying to do and it's not working. Maybe we're more than business associates. Have you thought about that?"

"We're not exactly friends, though," Kate said quickly. "We're more than acquaintances, of course, but I really do think 'associates' is the right term to describe us." She stopped, chagrined to find that Steven was regarding her with open amusement.

"You have to put a label on it, don't you?" he asked. "You have to make sure all the limits are strictly defined so I don't get too close to you."

"We both agreed on those limits," she said shakily. "We both agreed it would be a professional relationship, nothing more!"

"Why are you so afraid of me, Kate?" His voice was gentle. "I don't want to hurt you. I just want us to be honest with each other." He reached out a hand to her but she backed away, folding her arms against her body.

"All right, let's be really honest," she said, challenge in her voice. "Where do you see our relationship heading?"

"I don't know," he said slowly. "That's the whole point, isn't it? There aren't any signposts along the way to tell us where we're going."

"So you don't want to set any limits," Kate scoffed. "That's the best escape of all because it means you don't have to commit yourself to anything."

"You're the one who's frightened, Kate. You behave as if any minute prison bars are going to come slamming down in front of your face. It shows in everything you do—the way you run your business—"

"Oh, no, you're not going to start that again." Kate moved down the sloping yard and grasped the handle of the lawn mower. Steven followed her.

"We have to talk about it," he said ominously. "I found your note asking for more money taped to the refrigerator. That was a nice touch."

"I wanted to make sure you saw it as soon as possible."

"I suppose you thought it would be easy to ask me for more money because you succeeded so well the first time. You want my help with no strings attached. It's another symptom of your fear that you'll lose control of your life."

"I've had enough psychoanalysis for one day," she said, "though it's been very enlightening. Thank you for explaining to me that independence in a woman is something abnormal and neurotic."

"You're deliberately misinterpreting what I say," he told her. "Gloria Nestor is an independent woman, and I admire that in her. But she knows how to use her independence."

This was too much. Kate started pulling on the mower. She was angry, but most of all she felt wounded. Steven had compared her to Gloria and found her lacking. She didn't seem to have any defense against that; it hit her too deep and hard. Oh, blast! Couldn't Steven see that she just wanted him to leave her alone? But he wouldn't give up.

"Wait a minute," he said. "You're dangerous to yourself." He took over the lawn mower and hauled it up the hill. She had no choice but to scramble up alongside. At the top, he stopped and surveyed the jagged strip of mown grass that marked her earlier descent. To his credit, he maintained a solemn expression.

"I think we'd better try another system," he said. She couldn't argue, although she would have liked to. Steven disappeared into the shed, which had scallops of trim that matched the house. After a moment he emerged with some rope. Rolling up his sleeves, he squatted down next to the mower. Kate watched the deft movements of his hands. He tied the rope at the base of the handle, then stood up again.

"All right, I'm going to be holding onto the rope to keep the mower steady for you. Move in rows across the lawn, not down. Definitely not down. Got that?"

"Yes, sir," she said acidly. He glanced at her.

"Good. Let's go." He pulled on the starter. Fortunately the engine had survived its tumbles and started right up.

Kate had to admit that Steven had devised a good plan. He walked with her as she mowed, using his rope to work against the machine's weight on the steep incline. She was free to make satisfying, even rows in the shaggy grass. And she was free to wonder what other comparisons Steven had made between Gloria and herself. Would Kate always come up lacking?

"I can't believe you need more money already!" Steven shouted over the roar of the engine. Kate turned and started another row. He moved right along with her.

"It's the house," she declared loudly. "I've never seen a place crying out for so much attention."

"There's a new coat stand in the hall."

"I know. Isn't it wonderful?"

"And a model ship on the mantelpiece!"

"It's an antique. Did you see the workmanship?" she called.

"Those aren't exactly necessities, Kate."

"I don't agree with you at all." She plowed on ahead, but Steven just kept right on with her at the end of that stupid rope.

"This is a lot more serious than I thought at first," he yelled over the engine. Kate mowed furiously.

"You hired me to do a job, Steven," she yelled back. "That's what I'm doing."

"Your business is in trouble, Kate. You have to face that."

She turned to retort, but then slipped and had to cling to the mower to keep from falling. The only thing holding both of them upright was Steven, straining at the other end of the rope.

Kate regained her balance. She reached over, shut off the engine and then plunked herself down in the grass. Steven took hold of the lawn mower.

"This is an expensive one," he said. His voice reverberated in the sudden stillness. Kate mopped her face with the red-and-green bandanna.

"It's also a good one. It will last you a very long time."

"Your assistant called me at the office today, asking if I'd seen you. She said she'd been trying to reach you all morning. She sounded almost incoherent."

Kate looked warily at him over the plaid bandanna. "Paula? I'll call her right back. I'm sure it's nothing. I was, um, out in the garden for a while and I couldn't hear the telephone."

"She kept talking about little tables and big cushions. And a Mrs. Clove who wants her money back right away."

"Cleeve," Kate muttered.

"What?"

"Mrs. Cleeve. That's who she's talking about. I apologize for Paula. She shouldn't be going on like that to you. It's an inconvenience—"

"She sounded pretty upset, Kate. I think she has good reason to be."

Kate stuffed the bandanna back into her pocket. "I can handle my own business affairs," she said tightly. Steven leaned against the mower.

"I don't think you can at all," he remarked.

She stared at him. "I've had enough of this. First you come out here and kiss me. Then you tie a rope to my lawn mower... your lawn mower—"

"You needed kissing."

Kate struggled to her feet. "I don't need anything from you, Steven Reid!"

He took a slip of paper out of his pocket and examined it. "Another request for money, with daisies printed all over it."

"Just tear it up. I'll do without it."

He gazed at her speculatively. "I think you do need the money, Kate. Rather badly, too."

"Not anymore." She searched her mind frantically; there had to be other options.

"I'll give you a check right now," Steven went on imperturbably. "All the money you need to finish the job. On one condition."

"I really don't want to hear this—"

"The condition is that you let me do some financial planning for you."

Kate brushed the loose grass away from herself with determination. She couldn't possibly let him do this.

"I have a policy, Steven. No one looks at my checkbook but me."

"Afraid of what they'll find?" he asked conversationally.

She sighed. "Look, when my father was alive, he never allowed my mother any power at all. So she'd take the checkbook when he wasn't looking, and she'd write checks without recording them. Once she even mortgaged the furniture to pay for our Christmas gifts. To this day she refuses to admit that it was all a subtle rebellion."

Steven started chuckling.

Kate glared at him. "It's not funny! It's pathetic."

"I think it's pretty funny. Sounds like there was nothing subtle about it, either."

"Well, *my* checkbook belongs to me," Kate asserted. "I don't have to sneak around trying to filch money out of someone else's. So there's no reason anybody has to look into my finances."

He straightened and shrugged. "Those are my terms, and I suspect you don't have anywhere else to turn. Just think of it, Kate. I'll supply you with enough money to buy everything you want for the house, along with a generous amount to cover your time. How can you refuse a deal like that?"

She clenched her hands. Oh, that look of satisfaction on his face. He knew he had her, all right. The house needed everything she could give it; that was why she was in this fix. She'd always been able to get by before, no matter how precarious the situation.

But she wouldn't blame the house. Steven was enjoying his power over her. She *knew* he was, even though his face was impassive now. He could dominate her senses with one touch, one kiss. But that didn't seem to be enough for him. He wanted to take over the rest of her while keeping his own self intact.

She tilted her chin. ''All right, Steven. You win—for now.''

CHAPTER SIX

STEVEN LOST NO TIME in consolidating his victory. First thing Monday morning he dragged Kate down among all the business houses of power on Montgomery Street. He wouldn't explain what he was up to, but escorted her firmly to a building of glass and cool green stone.

Far Horizon Enterprises, that was the name on the building. Kate didn't like the sound of it. She stopped in her tracks and resisted as Steven took her by the elbow.

"Remember our agreement," he said. "We can't stand out here all day, Kate."

"I'm moving," she muttered.

"It sure doesn't feel like it."

"This is a mistake—I won't let you do this to me!" But today Steven was taking full advantage of his financial hold over her.

"You don't have any choice, remember?" His eyes were as implacable as gray stone. Blast the man! He was behaving as if he owned her, body and soul. She already had enough complications in her life; for one thing, Mrs. Cleeve was becoming more intractable every day. Not only did the woman refuse to pay what she owed on her account, but now she wanted all her money back and every trace of French Provincial eradicated immediately from her house. Kate and Paula had managed to establish only a precarious truce with Mrs.

Cleeve. Kate was on edge, and it didn't help to have Steven commandeering her like this.

He prodded her through the gleaming doors of Far Horizon Enterprises. Her feet sank into lush, moss-green carpet as she brushed past a hanging plant and a forest-green room divider. The walls had a slight lemony tinge; all the pictures on them depicted leafy, tropical scenery.

"Everything's green," Kate said with contempt. "What kind of place is this?"

Steven ushered her into the elevator. The doors shut silently behind them, and they were completely enclosed in a box of jade green.

"I don't believe this," Kate said. Steven leaned against the wall next to her.

"Why don't you just relax and enjoy the ride?" he asked with a lazy grin. "You look like a prisoner on the way to the gallows."

"That's exactly how I feel," she returned.

Steven's hand gently clasped her elbow again. "Trust me, Kate," he murmured. "This isn't going to be so bad."

She gazed at his nubby tweed jacket, unable to pull away from him. Her heartbeat had quickened at his nearness and she breathed in the subtle pine scent of his after-shave. She needed all her defenses right now, and yet she just wanted to go on standing close to Steven.

The elevator glided to a smooth halt.

"Any last words before your neck meets the noose?" he asked. Kate sent him a venomous glance, which seemed to have no effect at all. The doors slid open, and he propelled her into a hall painted entirely in khaki.

Gloria Nestor was waiting there, very sleek in a safari-style dress of khaki green. Kate stared at her, perplexed and dismayed. She had not expected to see Gloria today, and she turned toward Steven for an explanation. But he offered none, gazing back at her unperturbed. It was Gloria who took over.

"Kate, I'm so glad you could meet with Steve and me," she said in her distinctive, throaty voice. "In a moment we'll explain everything to you. What a lovely jacket you're wearing." She smiled appreciatively at Kate's tropical-orange blazer, then led the way down the hall. Steven went on holding Kate to his side as they followed Gloria into an elegant, khaki office where jungle scenes leapt out from prints along the walls. A tiger snarled from his covert; an elephant reared his tusks to an African sky. Gloria swung into a chair behind her desk, looking like a huntress with her flowing black hair and scarlet mouth. What flawless skin she had, unmarred by even one freckle. A disturbing emotion filtered to the surface of Kate's consciousness—envy. She was envious of Gloria Nestor. Automatically Kate sat down beside Steven, appalled that she could be feeling this way.

"Kate, I've explained to Gloria that I'm your financial adviser," Steven was saying. She winced at his words. Financial adviser   he might as well have been a jailer! She looked back at him coolly, briefcase propped up in her lap.

Gloria demanded her attention again. "Yes, Kate, Steve and I have discussed some exciting options for your future. We believe that the first step is to introduce you to Far Horizon Enterprises." She reached across the desk and handed Kate a booklet that had a glossy green cover. "This is a profile of Far Horizon that you'll find very interesting," she said with conviction. "Go ahead—you can look through it right now.

You'll see that Far Horizon is a large, healthy firm. We develop real estate and we operate everything from art galleries to luxury hotels."

Kate didn't understand why Gloria was delivering this sales pitch. She flipped through the booklet and saw columns of revenue figures, photographs of Far Horizon employees smiling widely into the camera, an artist's rendition of a new green building soon to rise in Los Angeles. None of it meant a thing to Kate. She snapped the booklet shut and placed it back on the desk.

"It's all very exciting, isn't it?" Gloria asked. She seemed full of lighthearted energy and purpose, as if she were brimming with a delightful secret she couldn't wait to share. Her dark eyes sparkled. "Steve and I both feel that your company has a great deal of potential, Kate. With the right management it could become enormously successful. Far Horizon Enterprises can provide that management, leaving you free for the creative end of the business. That's why we asked you here today—to discuss the fact that Far Horizon is interested in acquiring Melrose Designs."

"Acquiring?" Kate echoed faintly. "Steven, what—"

"Just hear us out," he urged, and Gloria gave her a reassuring smile. The smile didn't convince Kate at all; she used a similar one herself on clients and suppliers who were being uncooperative.

"I know this may not be something you've thought about before," Gloria said. "Selling your business is certainly not something to take lightly. All Steve and I are asking is that you give the idea your consideration." Her low, soothing voice was so persuasive. And the way she kept saying "Steve and I" made the two of them sound like a cozy team working together for the sole benefit of Melrose Designs. Steven was talking that way, too.

"We've discussed this at great length," he said. "Gloria has been with Far Horizon for several years and has revitalized a number of small businesses. I think it's a good opportunity for you, Kate."

What Kate really wanted was an opportunity to slug Steven. She gripped her hands together on top of her briefcase.

"Steve is right. Far Horizon Enterprises has a great deal to offer if you come on board with us," Gloria went on in her low, seductive voice. "Financial security, prestige, unlimited contacts, all the right doors opening up. You'd be decorating the most exclusive homes in San Francisco. You see, Far Horizon can give you power...as much as you're willing to reach out and take."

Kate listened in a daze to this hypnotic recitation. The last words hung dramatically in the air, enticing her. She wondered for a moment what it would be like to have power, and to wield it as confidently as Gloria Nestor. But thinking about this was like trying on a hat that didn't fit. Kate didn't want power—only freedom.

"I'm perfectly happy with Melrose Designs just the way it is," she asserted, glancing at Steven's impassive face.

"Of course you are," Gloria agreed. "But think for a moment about the possibility of 'Far Horizon Designs.' Think about all it could mean. You'd go farther than you ever have before." Gloria took out a sheet of stationery and ran a jade fingernail along the top of it. "Just picture the words, right here. 'Far Horizon Designs.'"

Kate examined the logo: a lemon sun rising over fir-green hills. She could not imagine using this stationery instead of her own flower-embossed notepads. Every month she bought a different design; sometimes she was in the mood for violets, sometimes for a riot of tulips. But she would never be in the mood for these uniform green hills, so unlike the wonderful variety and color of real San Francisco hills.

Kate glanced up and found Gloria observing her closely. Gloria seemed very determined to convince her about all of this, and yet surely Far Horizon didn't need a small company like Kate's. What exactly was going on here? Gloria Nestor was like an exquisite emerald, different facets of her personality flashing out at different times. It was impossible to know which facet was the real Gloria, and what her true motives were.

"I'm going to keep my own business," Kate said steadily. "I've built something under the name Melrose Designs, something that speaks for itself. I'm proud of that and I don't want to lose it."

"We'd want you to go on feeling that way," Gloria answered smoothly. "You see, the Far Horizon name *more* than speaks for itself. You'd have every reason to continue being proud."

Kate started to argue, but Steven jumped in. "Kate might feel better about going with Far Horizon if she knew she could retain her present business location," he said.

"Yes, I know we discussed that, Steve, but I'm not quite clear on a few details." Gloria gave him a lingering smile before turning back to Kate. Now she was brisk.

"Let me see if I understand this correctly. Exactly what *is* your business location? The address for Melrose Designs is in a residential area."

"Yes, that's where I live. I save an enormous amount on overhead, and—"

"You run your business from your home?" Gloria made it sound as if Kate were fencing stolen goods from her apartment.

"It's very efficient," Kate said defensively. "Most of my work is done in other people's homes, and Paula files all the paperwork neatly."

"In *her* home?" Gloria asked.

"Her apartment. Yes." Kate's tone was belligerent, and Gloria seemed to realize that she'd gone too far. She switched into her soothing mode again.

"It does sound like a workable system as things stand for you now. You've been very wise to keep your overhead low. But if you join Far Horizon you'll have your headquarters right here in this building. Come along, I'll show you what kind of office you'd have. I'm sure you'll be absolutely delighted with it." She ushered Steven and Kate out into the hall again and pushed open the door of a large, windowless room.

Kate closed her eyes and opened them again a second later, but the scenery had not changed. She saw glassy-smooth khaki walls and plush carpeting in a darker shade of khaki. The one picture on the wall was expensively framed, showing a stark desert landscape—sand and pale green cactus. Two chairs were upholstered in stripes of pea-green and . . . khaki. Kate felt parched, as if she'd lost herself in that desert on the wall.

"Isn't it marvelous?" Gloria asked.

Kate couldn't say a word. She struggled against the wave of claustrophobia that swept over her, determined not to show any weakness in front of Gloria Nestor. But she couldn't seem to get enough air to breathe. She turned blindly toward Steven, and his hand steadied her arm.

"Kate and I have another appointment now, Gloria," she heard him say, his voice sounding very faint. "We have to be going, but we'll meet with you to discuss this again."

"Of course. You look rather ill, Kate." Gloria's voice also came from a distance. She sounded solicitous, but perhaps she was only worried that Kate would be sick in this immaculate office. Kate swayed a little, determined to keep her stomach under control at all costs.

"We really are late for our appointment," Steven said, his hand still supporting Kate. "You'll have to excuse us."

"I'll talk to you soon, Steve..."

Kate did not feel like herself again until she was outside, away from Gloria and propped up against the low wall that surrounded Far Horizon Enterprises. Out here the air tasted fresh and pure. It didn't taste like khaki.

"I thought you were going to faint right in my arms," Steven said with a concerned look. "Are you all right?"

She nodded shakily. "It was an attack of khakiphobia, that's all," she said. One of Steven's arms encircled her with its comforting warmth and she had to resist an urge to burrow against him. She stepped back so she could face him squarely. "I'm grateful for the rescue, but how could you do that to me in the first place?" she asked indignantly. "Springing Gloria Nestor on me!"

Steven rested an elbow on top of the wall. "I had to be underhanded about it, or you'd never have agreed to meet with her."

"Of course I wouldn't have agreed!"

"My point exactly," he remarked. "I know you took an irrational dislike to Gloria from the moment you met her. Without a little push from me, you wouldn't be able to see what Far Horizon can do for you."

"My dislike of Gloria is completely rational," Kate began, then stopped herself when she realized how ridiculous this argument could become. "I don't trust Gloria, that's all," she said. "And I can't forgive the fact that you discussed Melrose Designs with her behind my back. You act as if it's yours to sell!"

"Actually it was Gloria who first suggested that Far Horizon might be interested in acquiring you. She's been curious about you ever since I told her you were decorating my house."

"I'll bet she was curious, all right," Kate muttered. "She's plotting something and I'd like to know what it is."

"You're being paranoid," Steven said.

"Surely you can see it, too!" she cried in exasperation. "Gloria doesn't want me at Far Horizon, and at the same time she *does* want me there—badly. I'm sure it all has something to do with you, but that's all I'm sure of."

"Gloria's a businesswoman," Steven pointed out calmly. "There's only one reason she'd make a decision like this—because it would benefit Far Horizon."

Kate frowned at him, pressing a hand against her damp forehead. "I'm still trying to figure out exactly what Gloria does," she said. "So far all I can see is that she goes around snapping up little companies and feeding them to Far Horizon.''

Steven almost smiled.

"She doesn't abandon a company once it's acquired. She makes sure the transition goes smoothly for everyone, and she stays in charge of all the management decisions. Gloria's very good at what she does.''

"Obviously you think so.'' Kate was stung by the way Steven admired Gloria. His voice was always emotionless when he spoke of the woman, but he portrayed her as a paragon of the business world. Then another thought struck Kate, horrible in its implications. "Steven, do you realize what you're asking me to do? You're asking me to let Gloria Nestor be my boss! I'd go crazy having her order me around.''

Steven merely shrugged. "If you'd stop overreacting, you'd see how much Far Horizon could do for your career. Your financial worries would be taken care of, for one thing, and you'd still have a lot of freedom.'' He gave her a real smile now. "In fact, your first job for Far Horizon could be to redecorate your new office.''

"Oh, sure. Gloria Nestor would go for that.''

"I think you're judging her too harshly.''

"She no doubt has her good points,'' Kate said. "She *is* stunning.''

"What does that have to do with anything?''

"I don't know.'' Kate sighed. She wished contrarily that Steven would say Gloria looked like a horse, but there was no chance of that. "I just don't want to lose my independence,'' she went on more forcefully. "I kept my part of the bargain in all this. You said financial planning, and I've gone this far. That's enough.''

"We're only getting started, Kate.'' He straightened his shoulders, a forbidding glint in his eye.

"I won't let you keep manipulating me," she said.

"I'm trying to help you, dammit."

"I don't want your help. Or Gloria's."

"I'm going to hold you to our agreement, whether you like it or not."

She blew her breath out sharply. "I thought no matter what your other faults, at least you were fairminded."

"What other faults?" he asked. She turned and began striding away.

"Wait a minute. Where are you going?" Steven demanded, easily keeping pace with her.

"To work on the house."

"We came in my car, remember?"

"I'll take the bus."

"Just stop, will you? I'm not letting you go anywhere. You nearly fainted up there."

"I'm fine now. Go find someone else to manage!" She walked faster.

"Stop," he said quietly, taking hold of her arm. "I told Gloria we had another appointment. You don't want to turn me into a liar, do you?"

"We don't have an appointment, so you've already sinned."

"Wrong. We're going to lunch."

Kate stopped. Deep down she wanted to be with him. She did want to prolong their time together, no matter what.

"I know a place in Chinatown, not far from here," she said, despising her own weakness. She was even enjoying the proprietary way he held on to her.

"Good," he said. "I haven't been to Chinatown yet."

Kate was stirred out of that hateful submissiveness. She looked at him in surprise. "You've lived in San

Francisco all this time and you can actually say something like that?''

"I haven't done much sight-seeing. I've been too
busy," he said defensively.

"You're right—you have been. Follow me.''

Now he was in *her* territory. Kate led him into the
bustling streets, where even the streetlights were
crowned with their own fanciful pagodas. Tall, skinny
signs climbed up the tall, skinny buildings, announcing
a wealth of shops and restaurants. Steven paused to take
in the scent of spices wafting from a doorway and
looked up at a sign printed in both English and Chinese.

"I like this,'' he said, clasping her hand as they went
on walking. Kate recklessly tightened her fingers around
his. She took him down a narrow side street and into a
small diner. The owner, Mr. Dow, came forward to
greet her.

"Katie, it's good to see you," he said. "How is your
mother? A pleasure to meet you, Mr. Reid. Come
along, sit over here." He was Chinese, but spoke with
a musical Italian accent. His background was a mystery, and he seemed to enjoy his customers' speculation
about it. Kate suspected he fueled the speculation with
some outlandish rumors of his own making; the latest
had something to do with Gypsies. She grinned at him
and took the chair he pulled out for her. Steven looked
a little befuddled, not quite so in control anymore. Kate
was pleased.

Mr. Dow didn't wait for them to order. He brought
plates of ravioli, his famous fish salad and two steam-
ing cups of peppermint tea. Steven gave the tea a sour
look, but took a sip anyway. Kate went after the ravioli
with her chopsticks, finding that her unsettling morning had made her quite ravenous. Steven examined his

own chopsticks quizzically. Then he glanced at the checkered curtains, the gondola painted on one wall, the Chinese lanterns hanging outside. Shrugging a little, he picked up a fork.

A while later he loosened his tie and leaned back with a satisfied expression.

"I could get used to this city, if I were going to be here much longer."

"You're wrapping up business, then?" Kate kept her tone light.

"I'm trying to," he said, tracing a chopstick over the checkered tablecloth. "Lately I just don't seem to be getting as much work done."

"Too many dinners and evenings at the opera," Kate suggested. She expected a caustic retort from him, but instead he was thoughtful.

"Saturday night at the opera, Gloria brought a friend with her, someone from a big corporate law firm in Los Angeles. Seems I could have a partnership there if I wanted one."

"You told me you wanted to get back to the grass roots," Kate said in surprise. "You sounded so excited."

"Yes . . . I'm still considering that. A smaller practice, maybe specializing in family law. I've come up with some other possibilities, too, like going into criminal law, perhaps as a public defender." Steven's expressive face came alive as he talked. "Practicing law on a smaller scale is rewarding, Kate. That's how I started out. You're closer to people. You feel that what you do really matters."

She listened to him, his enthusiasm catching hold of her. He was a good and decent man, surprisingly idealistic behind the cynical front he sometimes put up. Kate felt an odd thickness in her throat, wishing suddenly that she could share his plans. She concentrated on re-folding her napkin.

"I think it all sounds wonderful, Steven. But I don't see how joining a big law firm will fit in."

"It would be a good step for my career—I can't ignore that."

"Gloria likes the idea, I'm sure," Kate remarked. Steven nodded, looking amused.

"Of course she likes it," he said. "It wasn't a coincidence that she just happened to bring her friend along that night. She's trying to be subtle about it, but she thinks I should go on to bigger and better."

"So you admit it!" Kate exclaimed triumphantly. "Gloria is full of plots. She—"

"Hold on," Steven said. "Stop exaggerating. That's just the way Gloria is. She's always thinking in terms of business deals, each one bolder than the last. It's one of the things that makes her so successful."

Kate took a bite of the white-chocolate ice cream that Mr. Dow had placed before her.

"Maybe there are other kinds of success," she said. "Become a public defender or go into family law, Steven. Forget about everything else!"

His chopstick made a forceful pattern of squares on the tablecloth. "Life looks pretty simple to you, doesn't it?" he asked. "As a matter of fact, *my* life was simple until you came crashing into it. I was going along just fine, living in a world I could understand, even if it wasn't perfect. Mergers, stockholders' meetings, women with the same drive and ambition as Gloria Nestor. But you, Kate, you're in a different world entirely, one you conjured up yourself. It's full of colors and dreams but not a single practicality."

Kate watched her ice cream melt. Steven didn't sound very approving of her. It seemed that Gloria represented his type of woman: sophisticated, successful, wielding business power with flair. He was right—Kate wasn't like that. She had her own style and she'd always been proud of it before. But now she found herself wishing intensely that she could be powerful, take the corporate world by storm. Maybe then she, too, would have Steven's admiration.

It was shameful, this craven need to please him. She despised the need, and yet it grew stronger every day. She had to fight it with whatever weapon she had.

"I'll never stop believing in dreams," she declared. "Impractical ones that don't have a thing to do with money or prestige. You have a few of those yourself, Steven."

"I'd forgotten about them until I met you," he said wryly. "And now they're more alive than ever. You have that effect on me."

"Maybe that's good," she said. "Maybe you needed to remember your dreams!"

"All this is making my life a hell of a lot more complicated than it used to be. I don't know if I want to throw out everything I've worked for. That means something, too."

Kate pushed her bowl of ice cream away.

"So you'll listen to Gloria," she said. "You'll go for bigger and better."

Steven hooked an arm over the back of his chair. "I'll look into this law firm in Los Angeles to see what it's like for myself," he said. "But maybe I'll keep my partnership in New York. Then again, maybe I'll open an office in a little town somewhere and grow apple trees on the side. I haven't made any decisions yet, but when the time comes, Gloria won't make them for me."

"Well, that's all I want," Kate said hotly. "To make my own decisions, without interference from you or Gloria Nestor."

"Your case is entirely different, Kate. You need structure, otherwise you'll lose the freedom that's so important to you. Far Horizon will help you to keep hold of your dreams, don't you see that? I'm going to arrange another meeting with Gloria so we can really talk about this."

"You know what I think?" she exclaimed. "I think you're trying to push me into this thing with Far Horizon because you're at a crossroads in your own life. You don't have the answer for yourself yet, so you think you'll come up with one for me. Well, you don't need to bother. Solve your own problems, not mine!"

"We made a deal," he said, his voice unyielding. "You accepted the terms and you can't back out of them now."

"You're forgetting something! I could never consider a decision this major without talking to Paula and Max. They're as much a part of Melrose Designs as I am."

"I agree with you. This opportunity is theirs, too, and we'll want their input." His affability was deceptive, she thought darkly. "Go ahead and talk to them," he went on. "After that we'll set up a time for you and me to meet with Gloria."

There seemed nothing more to say. Steven was the kind of man who always needed to be in charge, and he still had everything just the way he wanted it. He still held all the power in this relationship. They stared at each other across the table, and Kate struggled to keep herself from being swirled into the depths of his eyes. Their intensity shook her.

"Agreed, Kate?" he said softly.

"You know you haven't left me any choice! I'll talk to Paula and Max." She scraped back her chair and marched up to the cash register. Snapping open her briefcase, she pulled out some loose bills.

"Don't be absurd," Steven said beside her. "I'm paying for this."

"It was a business lunch. I'll pay."

"Of course it was a business lunch. You're my client now, so I'll pay," he said.

"You're *my* client—"

"We didn't talk about interior decorating. Besides, technically that's my money you're throwing around."

"I don't care. I'm paying," she stated.

Mr. Dow came up to the register and settled the dispute.

"It's on the house, Katie. No, you can't change my mind. Just say hello to your mother for me."

Kate felt deflated, but held out until Steven pocketed his money first. They walked in grim silence back to his car. They drove silently all the way to his house and parked behind the battered furniture van that Paula and Max drove for Melrose Designs. Still without speaking, they sat in the car under the shade of an oak. Sunlight flickered through the leaves, warming the windshield. Steven's hand rested on the gearshift knob; Kate glanced down at his strong fingers, which could be so surprisingly gentle. She swung her door open.

"I won't keep you any longer. Goodbye, Steven." She was halfway around the car when she almost bumped smack into him.

"I thought you'd be in a hurry to get back to your office," she said stiffly.

"I am."

"So . . . goodbye, then."

"Goodbye."

They stood looking at each other for one long, sunshine-shimmering moment. Then Steven strode back around the car, climbed in, slammed the door and roared off.

Kate sat down on the porch steps, watching dolefully as one of the carpenters carried some boards to the back of the house. She thought about Gloria's exotic beauty and graceful style; she thought about her own freckled nose and the way she bumped into things because she never looked where she was going. And suddenly she wanted very badly to surrender herself to Steven, to be swept up by his compelling strength. She'd follow wherever he led her, even if that meant joining Gloria Nestor's camp at Far Horizon.

Kate jumped up. She had to remember that she was fighting a battle with Steven, a fierce and desperate one. She couldn't afford to lose either her freedom or her heart to him. The best thing was to begin aligning her forces right away; she was going to need every bit of help she could muster.

She headed into the house to find her allies, Paula and Max.

CHAPTER SEVEN

MAX THOUGHT joining Far Horizon Enterprises was a great idea. A glob of periwinkle-blue paint flew off his brush as he waved it about in the corner bedroom upstairs.

"This Reid guy knows what he's talking about. We'd be making a lot of money. Lots of it."

"Since when are you so interested in money?" Kate asked, her eyebrows drawing together.

"I could save up more for college in the fall," he explained. "So when I start classes I can afford to cut my work hours down."

"Max, you wouldn't really be working for *me* anymore," Kate said. "You'd be an employee of Far Horizon's and they might not be so flexible about your schedule."

He pushed up the brim of his baseball cap.

"Maybe I'll work my way up in the company," he said. "Then I wouldn't have to go to college at all."

"Max!" Paula protested, raising her paintbrush in a menacing gesture. "Don't you even think about it. Of course you're going to college."

Kate turned to Paula, glad to have some support. But she was in for an unpleasant shock. Paula set down her brush and hooked a shining strand of hair behind her ear.

"This could be the answer to all our problems, Kate," she said seriously. "I can't tell you how worried I've been about our finances. It's not just Mrs. Cleeve, either. We're suffering a general trend toward chaos. We need to control it and at the same time inject some growth into the business."

"You sound like you just walked out of a pep rally for accountants," Kate complained. "I thought you liked being independent. Setting your own schedule, taking off when you needed the time..."

"Those are all the things *you* like, Kate," Paula said apologetically. Her voice started traveling up and down the scale the way it did when she was nervous. "I need some order in my life, and knowing when I'll get my next paycheck. It's nothing personal. Really, it isn't! I'm sorry." Paula's cheeks had turned pink; she always colored when she was agitated.

Kate looked at her ruefully. "Don't apologize, Paula. You certainly aren't asking for very much."

"You're not angry, are you?" Paula asked, still anxious.

"No, of course I'm not. I'm just going to have to do a lot more thinking about Far Horizon, that's all. I'm glad you both told me how you felt." Kate went downstairs to the library. She stood at the mantelpiece, lining up a new row of M&Ms in front of the antique sailing ship. She ate the orange ones this time, slowly and thoughtfully. It seemed that life was more complicated than she wanted to believe. All along she'd been living her own dream, thinking that it was right for Paula and Max, too. That had been selfish, especially when the two of them were so loyal to Melrose Designs. They had sacrificed a lot to keep the business going; how could she deny them the opportunities they would find at Far Horizon?

At the same time, how could she deny herself? Yes, it might be a relief to have a regular paycheck, to know she could afford another car when her poor Bug wheezed its last. But Kate wondered how well she would survive in a place like Far Horizon. She was afraid that she might wither and die there, like a plant uprooted from a forest to a desert.

She could see no answers to her questions right now. All she could do was turn to the old house for solace and comfort. She placed a hand on the lovely onyx marble of the mantelpiece, pressing against the smooth, cool surface until the confusion of her thoughts began to quiet down. Then she slipped off her blazer and rolled up her sleeves. Ignoring the fact that she was wearing her best skirt, she went to work stripping the rest of the wainscoting. Somehow she would figure out what to do about Far Horizon.

Kate's first strategy was simple: she stalled. The next morning Steven called her twice while she was working at his house, pushing her to set a time for the second meeting with Gloria. She changed the subject repeatedly, she argued with him—and finally she just hung up on him. Both times. She was irked when he showed up in person an hour or so after their last confrontation.

He was in a good mood, as if he enjoyed having a receiver slammed down in his ear. Dropping his jacket on the newel post, he took Kate into his arms. It was a dangerous thing to do, since she was holding a hammer and a packet of nails and wasn't feeling very friendly toward him. But he waltzed her through the hallway with expert ease, humming a song from a Fred Astaire movie. He was a marvelous dancer, and his arms were strong and warm. Kate leaned against him, quite breathless by the time they ended up back at the newel post. He was still humming in her ear, sending delicious vibrations all through her. Then he kissed the pulse at her temple and stepped back. She almost dropped the hammer on her toe.

"Isn't this better than arguing?" he asked.

"Yes. Definitely." But she narrowed her eyes at him with suspicion. "You're changing your tactics too fast," she declared. "You're trying to soften me up, aren't you?"

"I wanted to see you," he said. "Spur of the moment—just like that. I almost gave Mrs. Adler a fit of apoplexy when I walked out of my office and told her to cancel my appointments for the rest of the day. I can't believe I did that myself." He was beginning to look disgruntled, like a man waking from dream to reality. But Kate felt buoyant, as if he'd whirled her around the floor again. He had disrupted his entire schedule—all for her.

"Well, I was just tacking in some baseboards," she said happily. "The carpenters finished up yesterday, but they forgot a few details—not that I blame them. The one named Jerry has been quite distracted by Paula. She finally said she'd go to the movies with him..." Kate was babbling; she never knew how Steven was going to affect her. But he didn't seem to be listening. He looked at the empty paint cans scattered about, the box full of doorknobs that had been pushed into a corner, the dust rags draped over the stair rail.

"My life is like this house," he muttered. "Everything out of place. Are you ever going to finish one room? Just one room, that's all I ask."

"Don't worry," she told him. "Everything's in a state of flux right now. Eventually it will all settle in."

"Good Lord, you make my house sound like a cosmic whirlpool. Maybe the whole damn thing will be sucked into outer space."

Kate tried to distract Steven. She pointed to a corner that was very neat and tidy at the moment. "Don't you think you should have a grandfather clock over there?" she asked.

Steven gave her suggestion some thought.

"That might not be so bad," he conceded. "Not bad at all." He turned back to Kate. "We'll go buy a clock right now—what do you say? A grandfather clock that chimes every fifteen minutes until you want to stuff a sock in it. Can't have a house without one of those."

This was much more than she'd hoped for. She stared at him. "Are you serious? That's really what you want to do?"

"I have a limited capacity for this kind of thing," he said. "Don't press your luck by making me think about it too much."

"Don't think about it at all, then!" She ran upstairs to tell Paula she was leaving, then hurried out to join Steven at the Mercedes. He opened the car door for her and gratefully she sank into the luxurious seat.

"I know just where to go," she said, giving him directions. She glanced at him as he drove. "Listen, I'm sorry I yelled at you on the phone."

"Are you sorry you called me an interfering moose?" he asked gravely. "I really am trying to come up with a good deal for you, Kate. I'm negotiating with Gloria so that she'll give you all the freedom you need."

Kate sighed. He was changing his tactics on purpose, she was sure of it.

"I already told you that Max and Paula are interested," she said. "But can you guarantee that they'd both still be part of Melrose Designs, just as they are now? And there's something even more important. They should have promotion opportunities at Far Horizon."

"Gloria will be fair about that," Steven answered. "You don't need to worry. Far Horizon rewards hard work and initiative."

It all sounded so logical, so suitable. And yet Kate's instincts still warned her to run from Far Horizon as fast as she could. Gloria Nestor was not offering any of this out of the kindness of her heart.

By now they'd driven past Market Street to a shabby, down-at-the-heels area where tourists seldom ventured. At Kate's direction, Steven pulled up at a dingy little store on a side street.

"I thought we were going to a department store or something like that," he protested.

"A department store?" Kate echoed in disbelief.

"How else do you buy furniture? You need a clock, you go to the clock department. You buy the damn clock."

"Good grief, you don't shop for furniture the way you do for... for shoes. You have to know how to browse."

"I don't browse," Steven said. "We're going to a department store."

Kate swung out of the Mercedes. "Relax! You're going to enjoy this." Before he could say anything more she led him into the shop. It was a jumble of dusty paintings, murky wood carvings, old chests and bookcases, tarnished jewelry heaped in cracked bowls.

"What the devil?" Steven grumbled, just as a tall, skinny old man materialized from the clutter.

"My dear Kate," he murmured in a voice that was papery thin. "I haven't seen you in a long time. Where have you been hiding yourself?"

"Oh, Mr. Addison, I've been working on the most marvelous house. You'd love it. It's up on McClary Hill."

"Ah, yes, interesting area. Fascinating history. Fascinating." Mr. Addison smoothed a few wisps of hair across the bald spot on top of his head. His milky-blue eyes took on a faraway expression. "McClary Hill used to be a stepping stone for people struggling their way up the social ladder," he said. "They committed a great deal of architectural excess, even by San Francisco standards. They built their mistakes and then abandoned them for better homes."

Kate shook her head emphatically. "The house I'm decorating up there—it wasn't treated like that. I *know* it wasn't. I just have this feeling about it. There must have been a family who lived there for years and years and loved it. I know for a fact that someone named Eliza R. Hobbes used to live there. I'm dying to find out more about her. Have you ever heard that name, Mr. Addison?"

He smoothed his wisps of hair in the other direction. "No...no, can't say I have. That's the trouble with history, you know. So many names, so many faces escape us. So many lives..." He sighed nostalgically.

"It's not the famous people who intrigue me," Kate said. "It's all the other people who lived so richly and deeply, yet we don't know anything about them."

Steven cleared his throat. "I thought we were shopping for a grandfather clock," he remarked.

"That's exactly what we're doing," Kate said. "Mr. Addison, this is Steven Reid, my client. And this is Mr. Addison, who can tell you anything and everything you want to know about clocks."

"I believe I have a few in the back somewhere," Mr. Addison said, gesturing vaguely. "A few months ago I spotted a cuckoo clock behind one of the bookshelves, but I haven't seen it lately."

Steven was tensing like a spring wound too tightly, and Kate put a hand on his arm. "I hate to tell you this," she said. "We're going to…browse. Trust me and see what happens."

Steven groaned, but followed her further into the shop. It was long and narrow, with more and more treasures piling up toward the back. Steven poked his foot at a rolled-up Persian carpet and fought his way around a china cabinet.

"How can you find what you're looking for?" he hissed at Kate. "There are probably a few forgotten customers moldering back here."

"Just be ready for anything," Kate instructed him as she went to inspect a table carved out of tulipwood.

Kate poked and sifted and scrounged through the entire shop. Now and then she'd catch a glimpse of Steven, mysterious rolls of parchment under his arm or his tie flung back over his shoulder as he rummaged through boxes. He reappeared at the front of the shop while Kate was consulting with Mr. Addison over the counter. She hadn't stumbled upon a grandfather clock, but contented herself with other finds.

"Let's see… We're taking the writing desk," she said. "And the walnut bureau. Oh, and that pile of sheet music."

"Wait a minute!" Steven protested. "What do we need that for?"

"Why, we just do, Steven," Kate said patiently. "There are some wonderful old songs in there. Now, Mr. Addison, I think that's all. We'll carry a few things with us, but Paula and Max will be around with the van tomorrow—"

"The armchairs," Steven muttered. Kate turned to him.

"What?"

"The armchairs over there. We're taking those. And that set of candlesticks."

Kate raised her eyebrows at the hideous Victorian candelabra, but thought better of arguing with him. It wasn't difficult to prod Steven to the next little shop she had in mind . . . and the next one after that. The possibility of a grandfather clock beckoned them on.

Kate and Steven scrounged and explored together. Right in the middle of a heated discussion over the usefulness of a battered washboard, Kate realized how happy she was. Simply and purely happy. She was sharing her world with Steven. And she wanted to share so much more of it with him—regardless of the tortured expression on his face.

Eventually he took off his tie and left his jacket tossed carelessly in the back seat of the car. The front of his expensive shirt grew dusty from rummaging among tables and cabinets and bookshelves.

"That mirror. Those rugs," he said. Kate began to notice a glazed look in his eyes.

"Perhaps we shouldn't take *all* the rugs," she hinted.

"All of them," he said grimly.

"Well, Paula and Max won't mind making a few extra trips," Kate remarked. "They'll stop for ice cream or pizza every few hours. Max is six feet tall and still growing—he needs lots of nourishment to load furniture. Paula always has to go on a diet after she's spent a few days working with him.''

Steven didn't answer. There was an alarming glitter in his eyes now as he advanced on a shelf of flowerpots. Kate decided it was time to take action.

''Kind of addictive, isn't it?'' she commented, and led him out of this last store. He blinked, glancing around in the sunlight. He still didn't look quite himself.

''Lord,'' he said, ''are we ever going to find that damn clock?''

Kate knew that drastic measures were called for.

''Look.'' She pointed to a cable car that was loading up with passengers. ''You probably haven't ridden on one yet, have you?''

''No... I can't remember if I bought that model train set.''

''Yes, you did. I think you'd better come with me.''

It was a wild ride. The cable car was jam-packed, and Kate and Steven clung to the outside.

His arm came around her protectively. ''Don't worry, I won't let you fall off,'' he murmured against her hair. She didn't tell him that she'd been hanging out of cable cars practically since she could walk. Instead she nestled a little closer into the circle of his arm. They plummeted toward the Hyde Street Pier. Usually this sweeping view of the bay took every bit of Kate's attention. Today, however, she was attuned only to Steven's nearness. The shining blue of the water, the tang of salt air, the carefree dinging of the cable-car bell—all colors were blurred, all sounds muted as Steven's lips moved over her temple. His arm tightened about her, bringing her closer still. And then the ride was over. He swung off first and waited for her. She looked down into his eyes as she took his outstretched hand. They walked with their arms bumping companionably, and Kate gave herself over to the joy of being with him. Surely this once it couldn't hurt to let down her defenses. Why, the beauty of the day practically demanded it! The weather was San Francisco summer at its best: bright and warm but not too hot, the lightest breeze stirring around them.

Together they wandered into the Maritime Museum. Kate showed him her favorite model sailing ship, so painstakingly crafted she could almost see it cresting an ocean swell.

"Now I know why you had to buy a model ship for the mantel," Steven said, squeezing her hand. "I'm glad you did."

She led him to the exhibit of figureheads—extravagantly painted wooden ladies who were always ready to lift up their skirts and go sailing off into the spray. And there was a scrimshaw collection, fanciful carvings whittled out of whalebone by long-dead sailors.

"I've always loved these carvings," Kate said, sighing. "I can picture so vividly the men who created them. But I feel terribly sorry for the whales."

"You have a tenderness for all living things, Kate. It's one of the things that makes you so special."

She smiled at him, relishing his words. But she had one more thing to show him—the picture of hundreds of ships abandoned in the bay when all their crews deserted for the gold fields in 1851.

"This is still the city of romance and adventure," Kate told him. "It has been ever since the gold rush days."

"I believe it," Steven said. His fingers caressed the nape of her neck, and she found she wasn't able to think very logically.

She managed to find the way outside again, and they went to lean over a rail, admiring the old schooners and tugs docked at the pier.

"I always used to wish I could take off in one of those ships," Kate said. "I wouldn't care where I ended up—wherever the waves wanted to take me. China, Japan, Australia."

"I think I'd like to buy a boat someday," Steven mused. "A small oceangoing one I could restore. You're right—that's adventure."

They didn't talk for a time, enclosed in their own magic, even though a crowd milled around them. Kate turned and looked at the towers of the Golden Gate Bridge rising majestically beyond. The moment was perfect, a gift of beauty.

Steven put his arm around her, his hand warm on her shoulder. "Kate... I have an idea about Far Horizon, and I want you to listen to it."

"Not now, Steven! Please—"

"We've had such a good morning," he said. "We should be able to talk sensibly about this now."

She stiffened. "I was right, then," she answered. "This was a new strategy of yours. You thought you'd get me in a good mood by shopping for a clock. You probably don't even want a grandfather clock!"

He looked harassed. "It was your idea to begin with," he said. "Remember?"

"But the way you canceled your appointments today... You had something in mind, some way to soften me up." She was rigid with indignation now. Steven maneuvered her around so that she had to face him.

"Listen to me, Kate," he commanded. "Believe it or not, I *am* capable of spontaneity, especially where you're concerned. You . . . do something to me."

She stood at arm's length from him, unable to trust his words.

"Blast it all, Steven Reid! You planned all this. Don't try to deny it. I was really beginning to think today was special. That we could be together without you trampling all over me."

"Lord, you do have a gift for exaggeration," he said. "All right, I thought it wouldn't hurt for me to be a little more flexible and spend some time doing things your way. But I didn't stay up all night hatching a plot. I just had an urge to see you. Is that so hard to believe?"

She didn't care what he told her, or how he tried to explain it away. "You're worse than my own father!" she exclaimed. "At least *he* never tried to charm my mother. He was always his grumpy old self, barking out orders and expecting them to be obeyed."

"I wasn't trying to charm you, Kate—"

"Well, you did a darn good job of it, anyway. You had me going there for a while. Too bad it all backfired. You spent a whole lot of money on furniture you didn't want—just so I'd melt in gratitude and do anything you said."

He brought her toward him and she had to plant both hands on his chest to keep a distance. He scowled down at her.

"You're right, I didn't want two lamps that need rewiring or a treadle sewing machine that won't treadle. But I saw the way you looked at all that junk—like you'd just discovered an ancient Egyptian tomb. So I bought the damn stuff! I got carried away. How much criminal intent can you read into that?"

She was trembling inside, wanting to believe that the morning had been special for him, too. A time to be with her and savor her company, nothing more. She took a deep breath.

"Prove yourself, then," she challenged. "Tell me right now that we won't talk about Far Horizon or Gloria Nestor, not once the whole rest of the day."

His eyes were stony now. "I'm not going to try passing a test for you, Kate. I told you the truth. On the spur of the moment I decided I wanted to spend some time with you. And yes, I thought it would help our relationship if I showed you I could give a little, too. But I've come up with a compromise on Far Horizon and you're going to listen to it now."

She kept her hands splayed across his chest, resisting him. But he held her captive with little effort.

"Gloria already has a client who wants her house redecorated," he said. "It's supposed to be one of your first assignments, but I think I can convince Gloria to put it on a trial basis. You'd find out how you like working for Far Horizon before actually signing on. Nothing could be more reasonable."

It *was* reasonable, and Kate found that especially irritating. She relaxed her vigilance for a moment, arms slackening as she tried to think of a rebuttal. Steven took advantage of this, his own arms tightening around her until she was cradled against him.

"I'm only asking you to do an experiment with Far Horizon," he said next to her cheek.

"I won't—I won't agree to anything under these circumstances..." His mouth was leaving a trail of flickering heat across her skin, and she couldn't think straight. A balding man with wire-rimmed spectacles looked on with interest, fingering his camera.

"We make a good picture together," Steven murmured in her ear. "And I'm handing over all the money you need, don't forget. I'm living up to my end of the bargain and you have to do the same. Say cheese."

She clenched her fists, but they were wedged securely between her body and Steven's. She arched her head back and stared at him.

"You have me entirely under control, don't you?" she asked bitterly. "But that's all I'm giving Far Horizon—a trial, just like you said. Nothing more!"

Steven released her, but not before the camera had clicked. It was a Polaroid, and a moment later the man handed Kate the photograph that had scrolled out of it. He peered at her over his spectacles.

"Have a good day, miss." He walked off jauntily.

Kate looked down at the photograph as the colors deepened. There she and Steven were, locked in what appeared to be a lovers' embrace. But they were glowering at each other, and that ruined the effect somewhat.

Kate didn't know whether to laugh or cry. Maybe she should be doing both, because it was preserved forever now—this moment of capitulation to Steven.

CHAPTER EIGHT

KATE CLIMBED THE LADDER to Steven's attic, grumbling to herself. Everything was moving too fast with Far Horizon, for once again Steven hadn't wasted any time. It was only yesterday that he'd forced Kate to agree to a trial, yet he'd already arranged everything with Gloria. Just now he had telephoned from his office to inform Kate that her first command performance would be this very morning: she was to be at a certain address on Nob Hill in precisely two hours. Kate had banged down the receiver in his ear again.

She had only a few hours of liberty. She knelt before the clothes chest, lifting up the lid and taking out the burgundy ball gown. She had brought along a generous supply of tissue paper, and carefully began wrapping the gown to protect it. Her hands lingered on the soft folds; she remembered clearly the way Steven had kissed her here. The emotions of that day had not dissipated, but still clung to the musty, closed-in air. Already she and Steven were building too many memories together.

Kate fished the Polaroid photograph out of her pocket and held it up to the light. She looked at Steven's rumpled hair, his obstinate jaw. He was staring at Kate as if the very force of his gaze would compel her to submit to him. His sleeve was rolled up above the elbow, showing the strong muscles of his forearm as he held her close.

Kate's fingers tightened on the photograph, ready to crumple it. But she knew that wouldn't do her any good. Even if she cut it into a hundred pieces and threw them all away, Steven would still dominate her thoughts. She tucked the photograph safely back into her pocket.

The other dresses in the chest required her attention. She smoothed out the wrinkles as best she could, wrapping each gown in tissue. It was an enjoyable task and she stretched it out as long as possible. Toward the bottom of the chest she found a strand of pearls, a mesh evening bag, and a book with a plain blue cover... a diary. She controlled her eagerness as she opened it, for the pages were brittle and coming loose from the binding. An inscription was written in ornate script on the flyleaf: "To Eliza Rose on her eighteenth birthday—fill this book with your happy dreams." It was signed Aunt Sarah.

Oh, this was treasure indeed. Eliza Rose—surely that was Eliza R. Hobbes. Kate sat cross-legged in front of the one small window so that sunlight would stream across the diary. Her gabardine trousers would be all grimy now, but she didn't care. Dust motes settled around her as she began to read.

The first entries in the book were about parties, balls, the boys who courted Eliza Rose. Eliza's handwriting was bold and impatient, so scribbled in places that it was barely legible. She'd obviously been a restless girl who wanted something more than the endless parties chaperoned by her parents. She wanted adventure, and one day she found it. Kate bent her head closer to the diary, scanning the words that had been dashed off so excitedly:

June 30, 1920

Something wonderful happened last night! It all started out as a lark. I climbed down the trellis after dinner to meet Cora, and we sneaked off to the theater. The play was marvelous, absolutely scandalous, all about a man who steals wives from unsuspecting husbands. Cora kept hiding her head in a shawl, but I wanted to see and hear everything. The villain was so dashing, a hopeless rogue, but no wonder none of the wives could resist him!

It was awful when the curtains went down. I didn't want any of it to end. Cora nearly fainted when I told her we were going backstage, but I dragged her with me. All I wanted was another glimpse of the villain. And then he was standing right in front of me, still wearing his silk waistcoat and his powdered wig. I could barely talk, but somehow I managed to tell him how much I enjoyed the play. And he just looked and looked at me. He has very intense, very blue eyes.

He asked us to go for coffee with him. Cora refused, but it was just as well. Michael and I sat in the café for hours. He looks even better without the wig. Curly brown hair, going bald just a bit, but I like that. All he's ever wanted to do is be an actor. I told him he'd be terribly famous someday.

He'll only be here another week. But anything can happen in a week!

July 6

Mama and Papa are in a dreadful temper. They caught me sneaking into the house last night. Michael got safely over the hedge, but they know all about him now. It's for the best. They can't stop us. I love him. And I know he loves me.

July 29

Still no letter from Michael. But I know he hasn't forgotten me—no matter what Mama says! Is it possible she was ever in love? I don't think so. Michael has to finish the tour of the play, that's all it is. He'll write. And he'll come back for me.

There were no more entries in the diary. Only a dried smear of ink where perhaps a tear had fallen those many years ago. Kate examined the pages again, tantalized by the mystery. Had Michael ever come back? Or was he a rogue even when he wasn't wearing his powdered wig and silk waistcoat?

Kate leaned back against the wall, her hands wrapped around the diary. She wanted to find out so much more about the history of this house. It seemed that the old place had known many emotions—heartbreak and despair, but surely happiness, too. She hoped Eliza Rose had found her Michael again and that she'd been happy with him.

Not too long ago, Kate would have wished for something else entirely after reading this diary. She would have wished that Eliza Rose had created a happy and productive life all on her own, without waiting for Michael to provide it for her. Surely that was more important than anything else. How could Kate forget so quickly? She had started to change inside, from the very first moment she'd met Steven. But she didn't want to change, didn't want to be as vulnerable as Eliza Rose had been all those years ago.

Kate glanced at her watch and grimaced. Her time had run out. She put Eliza's diary back in the chest, laying the tissue-wrapped dresses on top of it. Then she climbed back down the ladder, brushed off her pants and straightened the shoulders of her blouse. She was as ready as she'd ever be for her induction with Far Horizon Enterprises.

A short while later Kate's Bug wheezed painfully up Nob Hill and pulled into the drive of a hulking, dark stone mansion. Steven's Mercedes was already parked there. Kate sat in her car for a moment, smoothing back wisps of windblown hair. Even Mrs. Cleeve's sprawling house could not compare with this imposing mansion. Kate suspected that her trial run with Far Horizon was going to be quite a job.

She slid out of her car, glancing about at the smoothly manicured lawns, at the evergreens and hydrangeas that had been severely pruned. They looked like men who'd had their hair cut too short at the barbershop. The flowers in the garden were lined up in perfectly straight rows, as if measured out with a yardstick. Kate wondered if unruly flowers were yanked up by the roots. She shuddered, then advanced up the steps.

Two stone statues guarded the doorway—knights in chain mail with ill-tempered faces peering out through their visors. Kate tried to ignore them. Before she had even raised her hand to the knocker, the door opened swiftly and silently. A young man in a butler's uniform gazed at her lugubriously.

"Yes, madam?"

"Hello! How are you today?"

He gave her a suspicious glance.

"Um, I'm Kate Melrose," she said. "I have an appointment here..."

"Of course. Please come in." He stood back, and Kate walked into the gloomy interior. The windows were draped in dark brown velvet; all the furniture was made of heavy dark wood. Kate skirted a monstrous coat stand. The thing reminded her of a gnarled old tree that had been struck by lightning. She half imagined she saw branches reaching out to grab her as she went by. Shivering again, she followed the butler down a hallway. His brown hair was cut to severe shortness, though one unmanageable shock stood up in back. Kate wished she had a beach ball to bounce off his head. He was too young to behave so sedately.

Before she could reflect on this idea any further, Kate found herself ushered into the drawing room. And there was Steven talking to Gloria Nestor, his head bent toward her. Kate bit her lip, feeling a stab of pure green, animal jealousy. Then her mouth quirked wryly. At least "green" was an appropriate word when thinking about Gloria. Today the woman was wearing a soft knit dress the color of shamrocks. It outlined her curves, but not blatantly; she looked feminine and businesslike at the same time. She was also perfectly groomed. Kate suddenly became aware of the smudges still adorning her trousers, and wondered if she had cobwebs in her hair from Steven's attic. Oh, well, she liked cobwebs.

Steven was regarding her sardonically. Her heart pulsed in her throat as she gazed back at him. Tension crackled between them.

"My," Gloria murmured. Kate wrenched her eyes away from Steven and tried to listen as Gloria continued after a pause, "Steve and I are both so glad that you agreed to give Far Horizon a chance, Kate. I want to introduce you to your new client, Miss Marietta Winfield.''

Kate glanced about the room. Gradually her eyes discerned a very small, very old woman huddled in the corner of a huge horsehair sofa. She gazed out fearfully as Gloria led Kate over to her.

''I'm so pleased to meet you,'' Kate said, sitting at the other end of the sofa. The horsehair prickled her legs, but she sensed it would be best not to shift about. Marietta looked like a sparrow that might go fluttering away at any sudden movement. Her gnarled hands were plucking nervously at her brown taffeta gown; the stiff material covered her primly from her fragile neck to the tips of her toes. Her gray hair was dressed in the elaborate fashion of bygone years, the coquettish ringlets and curls somehow fitting against the wrinkles of her face. She intrigued Kate, most of all because she seemed so reluctant to have this meeting.

''Miss Winfield, why don't you tell me about your plans to redecorate the house,'' Kate began, feeling her way cautiously.

But even this appeared to be too much for the old woman. ''Oh, dear...plans...'' Marietta's voice was like a rustle of dry leaves in an autumn wind. She said nothing more, her face looking pinched and worried.

Gloria had taken a seat in a chair close by. ''Yes, do tell us about your plans,'' she urged. ''Marietta's niece is quite thrilled about them, Kate. Brenda Farrell— surely you've heard of her.''

Kate nodded absently; she'd seen the name a few times in the society columns. She waited patiently for Marietta to speak.

"The furniture must go," Marietta finally murmured. "Even though it has been in the family for years and years..." She patted her hand gently along the arm of the sofa.

"Oh, yes," Gloria said. "Brenda has already chosen some glass tables and an organic sofa unit. Light and airy. She's encouraging Marietta to go for an uncluttered look." Her gaze zeroed in on a bookcase that was crammed with knickknacks. Marietta's small, gnarled hand lifted to her throat in a gesture of alarm.

Kate examined the room again, making her own assessment. Most of the furniture consisted of massive, ornately carved Victorian pieces, ugly but in superb condition. The few Hepplewhite items were a welcome contrast, with their simple and graceful lines.

Kate's gaze came to rest on Steven. He was standing at the one window where the draperies had been pulled aside, and his tall figure was silhouetted by the light. She couldn't see his features, but she could tell his attention was focused on her. She turned back to Marietta.

"Miss Winfield," she said, "I want you to forget about Brenda and the rest of us for a minute. Just tell me what *you'd* like to see here in this room."

"Why... I don't really know..."

"Kate..." Gloria said, a warning edge to her voice. Kate ignored her.

"I think I sense what the problem is, Miss Winfield," she went on. "You don't want your house turned upside down all of a sudden. But have you thought of a few new touches here and there? Perhaps that little rug in front of the fireplace could be replaced. Something with a hint of pumpkin, you know.

And how about a few lovely vases to display your flowers from the garden?''

Marietta's brown eyes were suddenly hopeful. "Yes...yes, that would do nicely. I'd much prefer that. If only Brenda would listen..."

"Just tell her exactly what you want, and exactly what you *don't* want," Kate said cheerfully.

Gloria stood up, anger flashing across her face. But a second later she was composed again. "Marietta, I think it would be a good idea if I started showing Kate the rest of the house," she said. "We won't take too long." She waited for Kate to follow her out to the hall, then motioned the way into another drab room and closed the door.

"What happened just now with Marietta was really my fault," she said pleasantly. "I made a judgment error by not explaining the situation fully to you beforehand. Brenda Farrell is one of Far Horizon's most influential investors. When she told me that she was helping her aunt redecorate this house, I promised to do all I could to assist her. As you can see, Marietta is quite indecisive—she needs the guidance Brenda's providing. I don't want to undermine that."

Kate ran her hand over a lace tablecloth, which was obviously a family heirloom; perhaps Brenda wanted to get rid of it, too.

"I can't agree with you, Gloria," Kate said firmly. "To me it looks like Brenda's forcing her aunt into a decorating job the poor woman doesn't want. Marietta Winfield would be lost if her house were completely done over. She needs stability and continuity."

"You've barely met her! How can you possibly know anything about her?"

"It's obvious how she feels," Kate returned. "You could see it yourself, if you'd only open your eyes."

Gloria gestured at a lamp shade with a rotting fringe of brownish red.

"Look around you, Kate. Surely you realize this whole place is pathetic."

"Given a free hand, I *would* change just about everything," Kate said. "But that's not the point. I have to respect the needs of my clients. With Miss Winfield I would move very, very slowly. I'm sure she does want some change . . . but just a little."

Gloria rested her hand on an ornate captain's chair. She went on being pleasant. "I think I had better repeat this to you, Kate. Brenda Farrell is one of Far Horizon's most valued investors and I don't want to alienate her."

"Does this house belong to her?" Kate asked.

"No, of course it doesn't. It belongs to Marietta."

"I suppose Brenda will inherit it someday," Kate said reflectively. "That would explain things. She's just getting a head start on her own decorating ideas."

The anger sparked back into Gloria's face. "Her motives are none of your concern! At Far Horizon that's another thing you'll have to remember."

"Very well," Kate answered. "But I'm not going to help Brenda Farrell make her own aunt miserable."

"Think about what you're really saying," Gloria instructed coldly. "Think about it carefully and perhaps you'll want to revise it."

"I'm saying that Brenda Farrell has no right to take over this house before it's actually hers!"

Gloria paced among the heavy, elaborate pieces of furniture that probably had not been moved in generations. She emanated a tension that jarred in this room where time had stopped.

"I wish Steve could hear you the way I do," she said. "Somehow you believe that you should never have to compromise. That takes a certain arrogance, but Steve thinks you're so independent, so unique. He wanted to make sure you didn't lose any freedom at Far Horizon. I've tried to accommodate him on that, I really have."

"Why?" Kate demanded. "Why do you even want Melrose Designs at all? I wish you'd explain that to me."

Gloria smiled contemptuously. "It's very simple, Kate. I knew that once you were at Far Horizon and competing in the real business world, Steve would see you're not so special, after all. Just a common, ordinary drudge like all the rest of them. You could never climb very far at Far Horizon. You see, it takes something truly exceptional to succeed in a corporation like that—an ability to follow the rules and at the same time reach higher than anyone else. You just don't have that."

Kate listened with quiet scorn. "It was all a lie, then," she said. "You didn't actually plan on giving any opportunities to Paula and Max, the way you promised."

"Of course I did, if they could prove they deserved those opportunities. My offer was legitimate—I do play fair. It's just that I knew you'd flounder eventually in spite of that, Kate. I didn't expect it to be so soon, that's all."

"I suppose you thought I'd be easier to control."

"I prefer to say that I direct my employees," Gloria answered. "They're allowed plenty of responsibility as long as they don't do anything to harm the company.

I'm known as a good boss. You would have found that to be true.''

Kate shook her head in disbelief. ''You play games with people, Gloria. You even play them with Far Horizon, using the company for your own private schemes.''

Gloria's mouth constricted to a thin line of crimson, yet her beauty remained unmarred. When she spoke next, her voice was sharp and chilling, all the soft throatiness gone from it.

''I never jeopardize Far Horizon. Believe me, I'd like to keep you on so I could prove to Steve how ordinary you are. I'd really like to, but I won't. You're out of Far Horizon, Kate. Out.''

''I never wanted to be in,'' Kate returned. ''I think you know that. But I would have surprised you. I would have achieved my own kind of success.''

Gloria seemed to be enjoying herself now. ''Too bad we'll never know,'' she remarked. ''And it's too bad we both want the same man.''

Kate recoiled from this last statement, but she kept her expression noncommittal. Gloria watched her. ''Don't be so reserved, Kate,'' she said mockingly. ''Why don't you admit you're in love with Steve?''

The words hit Kate with a jolt. In love with Steven! That was the last thing she needed. She'd been struggling against it all along. She turned away, but Gloria spoke again.

''Just remember, Kate—I'm going to keep on fighting for Steve. I'll do whatever I can to have him.''

Kate swiveled back. Gloria looked so striking with her scarlet mouth and flowing black hair, her aura of self-confidence. But Kate wouldn't allow herself to feel inadequate. Not anymore. She had her own confidence.

"Watch out," Kate said hotly. "If I ever decide to fight for Steven, you'll have a real opponent. Because to me he'd be more than just a prize for the winning—much more. He might like that for a change." She went to the door, flung it open and strode down the hall, her heels making a forceful tattoo over the floor. She didn't look to see if Gloria was following.

Steven regarded Kate speculatively when she entered the drawing room to make her farewells to Marietta. The old woman held out a hand. "I hope you will come to see me again," she said. "And we'll talk about the pumpkin rug."

Impulsively Kate bent down and kissed Marietta's wrinkled cheek. Then she hurried back down the hall, and the young butler had to run in order to open the front door for her. He looked affronted, and tried to smooth his one stubborn shock of hair.

Kate leaned against her car for a moment, then reached for the door handle.

"You were wonderful in there with Marietta."

Before Kate could move, Steven's arms had come around her from behind. He kissed the nape of her neck, right there in front of the regimented flowers. Her body yielded only momentarily to his before she twisted away.

"You have no right, Steven! Especially after the mess you got me into today."

He leaned imperturbably against her car door, preventing her from opening it. "What happened with Gloria?" he asked. Kate laughed rather wildly; she couldn't begin to tell him what had happened.

"Let's just put it this way," she said. "Gloria has decided that she can't control me, so I'm out of Far Horizon. She made that very clear."

Steven looked amused. "Not bad for your first day on the job," he observed. "You managed to win the client over and get fired at the same time."

"That's right. I'm through with Far Horizon. I'd like to go now. Please remove yourself."

"Look, Kate. You were so good in there with Marietta. You knew exactly what she needed. I'll have a talk with Gloria and see if I can't unruffle her feathers. Who knows? Maybe someday you'll be bossing *her* around."

Kate glared at him.

"I can't believe this! You never quit, do you? I don't want to boss anybody around, not even Gloria Nestor. And I don't want you trying to manage my life anymore!" Her voice trembled with anger and frustration. She gripped the door handle, trying to nudge Steven aside. His body was rock solid, immovable.

Just then Gloria strode down the walk from the house, moving with easy grace. "I didn't have a chance to say goodbye to you, Kate," she called. "I do wish you luck." She sounded friendly, as if addressing a sorority sister. She positioned herself beside the passenger door of Steven's Mercedes. "I'm sorry I kept you waiting, Steve," she said. "I'm ready for that lunch you promised me."

Kate swallowed, her throat like sandpaper. She waited for Steven to move, staring at his elegant, dark green tie. Green!

"Gloria needed a lift this morning," Steven muttered to Kate. "What the hell did you expect me to do?"

"I'm sure she contrived to need a lift."

"Kate—"

"She's waiting for you."

With an oath under his breath, Steven left Kate. She slipped into the front seat of her Bug, pulling her door shut and locking it. She watched as Steven opened the door of the Mercedes for Gloria. She saw the way Gloria's jewel-green fingertips lingered for a moment on Steven's arm. Then Steven went around to his own side and the Mercedes swung out of the drive.

Kate rested her forehead against the steering wheel. She longed for only one thing now—to stop the words echoing in her mind. But they would not go away. They repeated themselves over and over, like a tape recording of Gloria's cool, mocking voice: "Why don't you admit you're in love with him? In love with Steven..."

CHAPTER NINE

GLORIA'S QUESTION pursued Kate the rest of the week, until finally she knew she had to turn and face it head-on. This conviction came to her late Friday afternoon in the produce section of the grocery store. She picked up a grapefruit and gave it a vigorous squeeze.

Am I in love with Steven? she asked herself forcefully, almost defiantly. *Well, am I or not?*

She wanted to discover the truth, for that would be her only strength now—to know what was in her own heart. And yet no answer would present itself. Baffled, Kate tossed the grapefruit into her basket and pushed on to the broccoli. Maybe the problem was that she couldn't even give herself a definition of love. She tried to puzzle it out. Her parents had certainly shared something all those years—her mother constantly worrying about her father, knowing the meanings and nuances of every grumble he made. He had worried about her, too, so afraid that she would leave him someday to become a painter or a writer. It had been a strange sort of mutual dependency, but her mother called it love. And maybe it was, at least for her.

What about Eliza Rose? She had believed herself in love with Michael after only a week. Maybe that had been something genuine, too, whether it had lasted for a moment or fifty years. Who could know? And the

way Kate felt about Steven...that was a whole laby-
rinth of longing and confusion. Who could unravel it?

Kate sighed and looked down at the bunch of broccoli she was clutching in her hand. She stuffed it into a
plastic bag, pitched it into her basket and headed for the
checkout line.

The telephone was ringing when she let herself into
her apartment. She dumped her two bags of groceries
on the kitchen counter and grabbed the receiver of her
wall phone.

"Where the devil have you been?" Steven's voice
demanded. "I've been trying to find you. Don't you
ever follow a schedule?"

She frowned and began rearranging the collection of
magnets on her refrigerator door.

"Well, hello, Steven. If you must know, I had to get
my hair cut," she said. "And then I did my grocery
shopping. There was a special on cranberry juice."

"How much?" Steven asked, sounding disturbed.

"Only a dollar ninety-five a bottle," she told him. "I
bought two. Cranberry juice is really good for your
kidneys."

"That's not what I meant! How much hair did you
get cut off?"

"Oh." She brought a strand forward and examined
it. "I'd say about an inch. It was just a trim."

"Good," he said. "I like your hair long. It makes me
think of strawberries." He barreled onward. "I've been
calling all over to see if I could find you. First I tried
Paula. She suggested I look in my attic. She says you've
been spending a lot of time up there lately. My entire
house looks like Attila the Hun is camping out here, and
meanwhile you start holing up in my attic."

Kate twisted the telephone cord around her finger. She'd been going up there to search for clues to the story of Eliza Rose and Michael. She hoped Steven hadn't noticed all the loose floorboards she'd pried up, looking for a possible cache of love letters.

"And then I phoned your mother," Steven went on. Kate pulled on the cord, cutting off the circulation to her finger.

"My mother!" she exclaimed. That was going too far.

"We had a very enjoyable conversation," he said. "She invited both of us for dinner tonight. I'll pick you up at seven."

"Oh, no, you can forget that," she declared. "We aren't going to my mother's house, for dinner or anything else."

"What are you afraid of, Kate?"

"Nothing. It will be a disaster, that's all. You don't realize what you're getting yourself into. I never know what my mother's going to say or do next."

"I'm willing to take the risk," he answered. "I'm intrigued now. I wouldn't miss this for anything."

Kate's hand tightened on the receiver. As if he could see her, Steven's voice took on a warning tone. "Don't even think it, Kate. You're not going to hang up on me again."

She relaxed her grip only with a great deal of effort, and scowled down at the receiver. "Steven, why was it so urgent for you to talk to me in the first place?"

"I had a meeting with Gloria today and we settled everything. She still wants you at Far Horizon."

"That can't be possible!" Kate protested. "Gloria was furious about the way I handled Marietta Winfield."

"As it turns out, Marietta refuses to deal with anyone but you. What do you think of that?"

"Steven, you don't know what went on that day between Gloria and me . . ."

"It doesn't matter what happened," he said. "Apparently it's quite a surprise for Marietta to stand firm like this, and her niece is backing her up. This is the time for you to sign with Far Horizon, Kate. Gloria will have to agree to your terms—she won't have much choice. You can call your own shots now, and you've accomplished that just by being yourself. That's really something."

Kate listened to Steven's voice. It was deep and vibrant, sending a current of warmth over the line. She found herself caught up in that current. It seemed she still had a chance to give Paula and Max all the opportunities they deserved. Paula had even been making progress with Mrs. Cleeve; she was developing public-relations skills that would make her a success anywhere—even at Far Horizon. Oh, it was tempting to think about proving Gloria wrong. Kate fantasized about it. She and Paula and Max would sail into Far Horizon, and they would succeed magnificently. There wouldn't be anything ordinary about it. After a while Steven wouldn't even look at Gloria Nestor.

Kate put a hand on the counter, trying to ground herself again. But nothing seemed clear anymore. Nothing at all. All her moorings were slipping away.

"Are you still there, Kate?" Steven asked softly.

She cleared her throat. "Yes, I'm here. But I'm not ready for any more pressure from you! Can't you understand that?"

"Actually that's something else I want to talk to you about." He spoke slowly, as if grudging his words.

"Kate, you've lived up to our deal. In all fairness I can't use it as leverage against you anymore. I gave you the money you needed; you gave Far Horizon a trial. We're even as far as that goes."

"Well, I'm certainly glad to have that off my back," Kate said fervently. This was indeed cause for celebration. She fished a carton of banana yogurt from one of her grocery bags, peeled off the lid and sampled a spoonful. "Steven, you're sounding almost like a reasonable man. Now at least you realize that this is my decision. Not yours, not Gloria's. Just mine."

"It doesn't mean I'm going to stop trying to convince you," he said, sounding cantankerous. "I still think Far Horizon is a big break for you, and I'll do everything I can to make you see that."

Kate licked her spoon. "I'm going to consider Far Horizon very carefully," she answered. "But I'm not going to make a decision right away."

"You can't delay too long, Kate. You won't have this opportunity forever."

"I'll keep that in mind," she said patiently. "Goodbye now."

"Don't forget—I'm picking you up at seven." This time he hung up first, and in quite an abrupt manner. Kate stirred her yogurt and ate it absently. From now on she was going to be much more frugal with money; anything was better than giving Steven financial power over her. She was free of it now, and she meant to remain free.

But that didn't change the fact that she needed to make a decision about Far Horizon. She wanted it to be an intelligent and logical one, but her feelings for Steven kept intruding and confusing her. Worst of all, she wasn't even sure what those feelings were. Love, desire, need?

Steven had made life even more complicated by arranging that dinner tonight with her mother. He seemed determined to go through with it, however; if he was going to be so stubborn about it, he might as well suffer the consequences.

Hurriedly Kate put away her groceries, cramming boxes and cans into the cupboard and shoving everything else haphazardly into the fridge. Next she drew herself a bath in her big, old-fashioned claw-footed tub. This was always a good therapy technique. Sometime later she emerged from the tub with flushed skin and pruny toes, slightly more resigned to the experience ahead.

Wrapped in a flannel robe, she attacked her closet for something to wear. What about her navy-blue slacks? No, they weren't right at all. She could always count on her turquoise dress, of course, but Steven had already seen her in it....

Kate stopped herself. What was she trying to do, sweep Steven off his feet? Ridiculous! She liked to get as much use as possible out of her clothes, regardless of male opinion. Nevertheless she rejected the turquoise dress and slipped it back on the hanger, pushing it to the far side of the closet.

At last Kate pulled out a dress she'd bought in a fit of extravagance but had never worn. It was a rich ivory, with narrow straps at the shoulders and a gored skirt that flared out in just the right way. Kate slipped into it. She lifted back one side of her hair with a tortoiseshell comb and allowed the rest to fall loose. Just a touch of lip gloss now, and a little mascara. Kate surveyed herself in the mirror. It would have to do.

Steven arrived promptly at seven, his arms full of violets for Kate. Laughing with delight, she gathered them into her arms.

"Oh, thank you, Steven. You must have bought out an entire shop," she exclaimed.

"It was a man, standing on a corner with a wooden tub full of violets." He grinned, the corners of his eyes crinkling. "They made me think of you, spilling out all over everything and looking beautiful."

Kate was touched by his words, and lowered her cheek to the violets. Then she busied herself finding vases for them, calling upon some empty jars, as well. She observed her arrangements with satisfaction; violets in old jam jars were very pleasing to the eye.

Steven came over to her.

"Now you make me think of seashells," he murmured. He lifted his hands to her bare shoulders, his skin against hers. Without thought or question she raised her face. His mouth captured hers with sweetness, enticing her response. She clung to him, parting her lips to his long and tender kiss. When finally they broke apart, Steven's eyes had darkened to a smoky gray.

"If we keep on like this, we'll never make it to your mother's," he said wryly. "She happens to be expecting us."

Kate nodded. She moved unsteadily to the hall closet and began hunting for her shawl. Meanwhile Steven surveyed her apartment.

"This place is suffering a personality crisis," he pronounced.

Kate poked her head around the door of the closet. "What do you mean?"

"Look over there. You have a desk made out of plastic cubes, some dead branches sticking out of a silver vase and a painting that can only be called minimalist art."

"Well—"

"On the other hand, over here you have two antique bookshelves and a sampler that says, Keep Your Candle Bright. Hmm. I kind of like that."

"I've gone through some different stages," Kate defended herself. "I'm still trying to, um, synthesize everything."

Steven put his hands into his pockets and wandered around the living room.

"You know, Kate, you were right that day when you told me I've been looking for a home without really knowing it. For years I've been caught up in my career, neglecting everything else. All the women I've known . . . they've been like that, too. You're different—you know how to savor life. But you don't have a real home, either. You're just as bad as I am."

"That's not true!" she said indignantly. "I've lived here for years. I've established myself—"

"Looks like you haven't even unpacked yet." He picked up a calendar that was two years old.

"I'm saving that for a reason," Kate said, taking it from him and stuffing it into her carved wooden magazine rack from Iceland. She rummaged in the closet again. All right, she didn't have much time to spend decorating her own apartment; all her efforts were expended on other people's houses. But Steven was wrong. She already *had* found a home—the house on McClary Hill. Unfortunately, she didn't really belong there; her stewardship of the place was only temporary. Still, there was every chance that Steven wouldn't be staying in San Francisco; he might take that position in Los Angeles. Then maybe she could find a way to buy the house—or rent it from him. But the thought of his not being in San Francisco was a bleak one.

She reached out and fumbled with windbreakers and sweaters, at last finding her shawl tucked among them. Woven in a soft shade of fawn, it was a perfect match for the strappy, high-heeled sandals she was wearing. Steven helped drape the shawl over her shoulders, then smiled down at her. They went out the door together.

Kate wasn't used to wearing such frivolous shoes, and had to use Steven's assistance as she navigated the two flights of stairs, which were very narrow and very steep.

"These steps were made for small, nimble Victorian gentlemen," Steven observed. "I wonder how Victorian ladies climbed them, having to contend with all those long skirts and bustles."

Kate welcomed his light tone. "Thank goodness times have changed," she said, then almost twisted her ankle. She looked down at the spindly heels of her sandals. "Now we women torture ourselves strictly by choice. That's progress," she concluded philosophically.

"You have pretty feet, Kate. I think they'd look good even in combat boots." Steven held on to her until he had deposited her safely in the Mercedes.

They arrived at Lorna Melrose's door, and she flung it open wide to receive them. She was wearing a new housecoat bright with gigantic cabbage roses, and her usual slippers had been exchanged for shoes that squeaked. She and the kittens crowded into the doorway to greet their dinner guests.

"Katie, Mr. Reid! How wonderful that you could come."

"Please call me Steven."

She gave him a broad smile. "Come along, then. The stew is almost ready." She bustled and squeaked down the hall. Kate followed, nudging at a ball of yarn that was unraveling all over the floor. A kitten pounced on the yarn before a path could be cleared for Steven, but he merely scooped the kitten up. Two paws dangled awkwardly from his hand and immediately a small engine began to purr.

Lorna waved Kate and Steven into chairs by the kitchen table. "No, no, Katie, you're to sit there and relax. I don't need any help. Everything will be ready before you know it."

Kate sat down and smoothed out her dress, glancing at Steven. His subdued but expensive clothes seemed more suited to dining aboard a corporate jet or a yacht. That tweed jacket certainly hadn't been made for a fusty little kitchen with cracked linoleum and faded curtains. But Steven leaned back comfortably in his rickety chair, the kitten perched on his knee. It hadn't stopped purring.

"Tell me about yourself, Steven," Lorna Melrose said as she peered deep into the battered, enormous old pot on the stove. She slammed the lid back on as if to prevent something from escaping. "Tell me about your home in Vermont, your family. What do your parents do? How many brothers and sisters do you have? Are you the youngest, the oldest, or in the middle somewhere?"

"Well, let's see..." Steven answered each question in order, not showing even the slightest annoyance at this interrogation.

Kate frowned down at the nicked surface of the table. She had to jump back as bowls and plates began clattering onto it. A pewter mug went spinning past her;

Steven caught it neatly before it could sail off the table. Kate stood up and took charge of the silverware before it could become a danger to anyone. Lorna squeaked about happily.

"There! You see, we're all ready. Have a biscuit, Steven. Have two. Dear me, I thought I went for butter yesterday..."

"I'll find it, Mother." Kate poked gingerly in the refrigerator. She saw two or three containers that it would be safer not to investigate. And what was that? she wondered at the oddest shape bulging in foil. Kate withdrew her fingers hastily. She found the plastic butter keeper at the very back of the fridge. The butter inside it *looked* fresh. She placed it on the table and watched Steven have a go at her mother's heavy, filling biscuits.

The stew was also heavy and filling. Kate prodded at the chunks of potato and carrot with her spoon while Steven and Lorna talked.

"Youngest but one, are you?" Lorna said. "That's a tricky position to be in. Now, if you're the oldest, your parents make a fuss about every little thing you do, like you were the first baby ever born. If you're the youngest, they take too many things for granted. They've seen it all before. And if you're next to the youngest, it's almost as bad. It means your parents were winding down when they had you but couldn't exactly decide when to quit."

Steven chuckled. "I believe you've pegged it, Mrs. Melrose—"

"Call me Lorna."

"Lorna. But the youngest in my family is a girl. My parents didn't take that for granted, after five boys."

"It's good you have a sister. Boys need sisters. Don't you think so, Katie?"

Kate started. "Oh...yes, sisters. Absolutely." She stared down at the stew that had been served at this table for as long as she could remember, usually on Saturday nights.

"Kate tells me you're quite an artist," Steven said.

"Goodness. Well, Katie has great faith in me." Lorna dished Steven up another bowl of stew and sent it sailing over to him. Fortunately he had very good reflexes, or it would have landed in his lap. "I always wanted to be a painter, you know. I just never had the time. Husbands require even more attention than children, if you're really going to do things right. And now I have all these grandchildren..."

Kate watched as Steven nodded sympathetically. She set down her spoon and pushed her bowl away. Out came the blueberry pie now, her mother's other dessert besides custard. The crust was thick and substantial. Kate knew exactly how the pie would taste even before she took a bite. Delicious but just a little too sweet. Heavy whipped cream on top that wasn't sweet enough.

Steven didn't bat an eyelid when one of the kittens finally made its move, springing from the counter onto the table. Lorna waved her arms, nearly swatting Steven.

"Shoo!—shoo! Where are your manners? Down with you!"

Kate snatched the kitten and leaned down to tuck it between her feet so it couldn't get away.

"Have another piece of pie, Steven," Lorna said. "Go ahead. There's plenty!"

By now even Steven was beginning to flag. "Thanks, but I don't really think I can fit it in—"

"Of course you can. Just a small piece." She sent a slab of pie across the table at him. He dug in manfully.

The kitten was wriggling its way out from Kate's feet. Meanwhile another one was stalking across the counter.

"Why don't we move into the living room?" Kate suggested.

"That's a good idea, Katie." Lorna's face was rosy and happy under her flyaway mop of hair. "We'll drink some peppermint tea. Have you ever tried it, Steven?"

"Yes, I have." He threw Kate an acid expression. She glanced away.

"Maybe Steven would rather have coffee," she told her mother.

"No, no—peppermint tea is fine," he said.

The living room had been shut up for so long that the air smelled stale. Piles of old magazines and newspapers sat in the corners, jars of dead plant cuttings on all the tables. Lace doilies sprouted in profusion on the chairs and sofa.

Steven joined Kate on the too-soft, squat old sofa, his knees sticking up. Lorna plunked herself in the rocking chair.

"Goodness, I'd forgotten about this." She picked up a narrow, straggly length of knitting still hanging from its needles. "I wonder what I was trying to make," she said as she started knitting. "So. Why haven't you ever married, Steven?"

"Mother!"

"I guess the right girl has just…never come along." Steven's gaze roved over Kate.

"Oh, but you can't sit around waiting for the right person," Lorna said cheerfully. "You have to go out looking. That's what I keep telling Katie. But you two haven't done too badly for yourselves. Not badly at all.''

Color stained Kate's cheeks. Lorna just went on rocking madly and knitting, a calico kitten perched on her shoulder. Steven just sat there looking perfectly comfortable in spite of the absurd angle of his knees. How could he seem so at home? Kate herself had never felt she truly belonged in this house. Always she'd been restless, eager to get away and find the beauty she longed for. This was a part of her life that she'd left far behind—and she didn't want Steven to have anything to do with it.

Kate struggled up from the sofa, drawing her shawl tightly around her shoulders.

"We have to go now," she said. "Thank you for the dinner, Mother. It was simply . . . lovely.''

"We have plenty of time," Steven countered, settling back more comfortably. Kate stared at him.

"We have to go right now," she said. "At least I do. If you'd prefer to stay, I'll just take a cab.''

Steven's mouth twitched, but he fought his way up from the depths of the sofa.

"I guess the night is slipping away faster than I thought," he said in a serious tone.

Lorna went right on rocking, her knitting needles flying. But she had watched this exchange with hazel eyes that were altogether too quick and bright.

"We'll let ourselves out, Mother.''

"Oh, no, I can't have that." With a squeaking of shoes and a mewing of kittens, Lorna led the way to the door. "I'm so sorry you have to leave, but you will come again, won't you, Steven?''

"Of course. I had a delightful evening." He shook her hand gravely.

Outside Kate headed for the car, but Steven placed a hand on her arm. "Let's take a walk after that dinner. What do you say?"

"Fine." She turned and went the other way. "Don't tell me you're complaining about my mother's cooking," she threw over her shoulder.

"Not in the least." He kept pace with her easily. "I always enjoy a walk after a good meal."

"Well, that's fine. Just wonderful." She lengthened her stride, but Steven barely had to accelerate.

A little boy bounced a ball on one of the stoops; three girls played hopscotch in the light thrown from a window onto the sidewalk. Rock music blared from a car parked down the street. All the houses were the same—squat, ugly, shabby, even in the dark.

"You know," Steven remarked, "any other woman might be happy for a man to like her mother."

"I'm glad you like her. The two of you should set up shop together."

"What's wrong, Katie?"

"Nothing! And don't call me that."

He shrugged mildly. They went on walking. The silence between them was covered up by the rock music and by the shouts of children. At the corner Kate turned back.

"I just want to go home," she said.

"She's not so bad, you know. She's a lot like you, as a matter of fact."

Kate pulled herself up short. "Mother and I aren't a bit alike!"

"On the contrary. Maybe if you admitted that, you could make peace with her."

"I suppose after one dinner you know all about it," she retorted. "You think you can just waltz into my life and sum it all up!"

"I'm fair at a waltz," he said, "and I've rebelled against my own parents, just like everybody else."

"Oh, wonderful." Kate went on walking. "Chalk it up to a little rebellion left over from my teens. Didn't you hear her? She said she doesn't have time to do anything with her life. She's always said that, always. And now I know that she'll keep on saying it." At last Kate understood something. She looked up at Steven. "Don't you see?" she asked. "My father tried to control my mother. He didn't want her to be an artist, to do anything that excluded him. But he's not stopping her anymore! Now it's just her, always making more excuses. No matter how domineering my father was, she's the one responsible for wasting her own talents. No one but her."

This fact was so basic, so utterly simple, but she had never realized it before. All this time she had blamed her father for holding Lorna back. She had imagined him with a power far greater than he'd actually possessed; the truth was that Lorna had created her own life, molded it to her own satisfaction.

Steven was gazing down at Kate in the pool of light cast by a street lamp.

"I think you're being too hard on both your parents," he said. "If you could just accept them—both of them—you'd be able to let go of your anger."

Kate stood very still. "Steven, I'm ahead of you on this," she said. "Tonight I've really seen my parents—the way they actually were together, not the way I always remembered them. I don't know if that's acceptance, but it does mean letting go, at least a little." She felt she'd taken a step into the future—her own future, not a repetition of the life her parents had lived. But that was more frightening than anything she'd ever done before. Without the past to cloud her vision, she could see Steven so clearly now. She could see herself, and the way she felt about him . . .

She wasn't ready, after all! Not for this, not for the stark, elemental knowledge that she loved Steven. She made a desperate struggle against it.

"Please take me home," she said. She went to the Mercedes, wobbling in her blasted heels. Steven caught hold of her arm.

"What is it, Kate? The look on your face just now. What's wrong?" He was being gentle. Oh, damn, he was such a wonderful, endearing mixture of tenderness and stubbornness, idealism and hard practicality.

"Don't ask me any more questions, Steven," she begged. "Just take me home!"

He obliged her this time, and they maintained a strained silence during the drive. When he pulled up in front of her place, she wouldn't let him come inside. Down in the foyer she unstrapped her shoes and ran barefoot all the way up the stairs. At the top she shut her door and locked it and pressed shaking hands against her cheeks. She looked at the profusion of violets. And she knew she couldn't lock Steven out of her heart or mind.

She loved him. She was deeply and irrevocably in love with Steven Reid.

CHAPTER TEN

KATE TRUDGED UP THE WALK to a castle on McClary Hill. Granted, it wasn't a very large castle, but it had turrets and towers everywhere in mossy gray stone. A small pond even served as a moat, the pathway turning into a bridge to cross it. Kate stopped for a moment to look down into the dark green water, her throat parched with thirst. She had been traipsing up and down Mc-Clary Hill all day, trying to find anyone who might know the history of Steven's house. The whole time her eyes had welled with tears—being in love was turning out to be a very briny experience for her. She hadn't slept at all last night, not after that revelation of her love. She couldn't confide it to anyone, least of all to Steven. He was attracted to her; she was sure about that much. But that didn't mean he would ever love her.

She didn't want to love him! She wanted her old, carefree self back. She'd been so happy and independent before she met him. What was going to happen to her now? She couldn't seem to stop crying.

Two ducks paddled by in the pond below and quacked a belligerent greeting at her.

"Hello, yourselves," she croaked back. She crossed the bridge into a wild garden where roses, daffodils and pansies all tangled together. Kate lifted the knocker on the massive wooden door.

There was no response after several knocks. She turned dispiritedly to go, but then the door creaked open. She turned back to find a large, loose-limbed man regarding her from under a shaggy thatch of white hair. He had a big, friendly nose and faded blue eyes enmeshed in wrinkles. His enormous, baggy overalls matched the shade of his eyes, and bristled with all sorts of intriguing pockets.

"Good afternoon," he boomed. "What can I do for you?"

"Good afternoon. I was hoping to speak to the owner of the house."

"That's me! That's me, all right. Lord of the manor." His laughter rang out. It was infectious, and Kate smiled back weakly. "Come in, come in, young woman, and tell me what I can do for you. But first you look like you need some refreshment. Will apple juice do?"

"Yes . . . thank you." Kate stepped across the threshold. The man shuffled away, leaving Kate to the scrutiny of an elderly beagle. Apparently she passed muster, for he gave a solemn wag of his tail.

"That's Fred," the man said when he came back.

Kate gave the dog a good scratch behind the ears and earned another wag. She stood up and gratefully took a chilled glass of juice. Sipping it, she began to feel a little less salty.

She glanced about the spacious hall with its high ceiling. The furnishings were sparse, but beautiful: oak chairs with simple, elegant lines; a sideboard with a delicately etched leaf design.

"These are wonderful," Kate murmured, stopping to examine each piece.

"Like 'em, eh? You won't mind talking to me in the workroom, then." He and Fred led her through a warren of rooms out to a large, sunny porch. Wood was stacked neatly in the corners; sawhorses and racks of tools and workbenches were everywhere. Two chairs stood in the middle of the airy room, waiting to be finished. Kate delighted in the pure gleam of sunshine on wood, the clean simplicity of both the workshop and the furniture. Even the sawdust was swept into neat piles.

"My father was a carpenter, too," the man said. "Have a seat there." He pointed out a stool that had the same clean lines as the chairs. "Built this crazy castle when he made it big in the construction business."

Kate settled herself on the stool and flexed her aching feet. She watched as the man took a piece of sandpaper from one of his pockets and began working a lovely piece of rosewood. Fred slumped down beside him.

"You've lived here all your life, then?" Kate asked. "You know the neighborhood?"

"That I do, miss, that I do. There've been Newberrys here for over a hundred years now."

Kate drew in her breath a little. "Mr. Newberry, have you ever heard of Eliza Rose Hobbes?"

"There used to be a Mrs. Hobbes up the hill a ways."

"Yes, yes, that's her! Can you tell me anything about her?" She clasped her hands tensely around the glass of juice. No one else in the neighborhood had been able to help her. Mr. Newberry continued sanding calmly and methodically.

"Well, now... she was a pretty woman. Always had a flock of children about her. Her own brood, along with the neighborhood kids like me. She made the best hard candy I've ever tasted." He chuckled in his deep bass, poking around in his pockets until he produced a packet of red licorice. "Like some?"

"Thank you. Then Eliza was married?"

"Yes. Mr. Hobbes used to order furniture from my father. A quiet man, he was."

"Do you know if his name was Michael? Was he an actor?"

"We just knew him as Mr. Hobbes. He was on the small side, with a big handlebar mustache. Never will forget that mustache. He used to play Santa Claus for us at the neighborhood parties."

"Can you tell me anything more about him and Eliza? Anything at all?"

"Let's see..." The sandpaper rasped in a soothing, constant rhythm. "She had dark hair and big blue eyes. Lively, she was. She had a beautiful voice and sang with the church choir. And that hard candy...oh, that candy makes my mouth water right now. Peppermint, that was the best."

Kate gave a slow, deep sigh and chewed thoughtfully on her licorice.

"Her daughter Lucy could tell you everything you want to know," Mr. Newberry went on. "Lucy Martin. Lives in San José, I think."

Kate jotted down the information.

"Thank you so much, Mr. Newberry. Well, I'll let you get on with your work now," she said reluctantly. She didn't want to leave. She felt safe and protected in here behind the moat.

"You look tired, young lady. Go ahead and sit a while. Solitary work, this. Glad for the company." He searched methodically through his pockets again and Kate watched, mesmerized. Some of his pockets were so small only a thumb could poke inside them. Others held pencils, nails and a hammer. At last Mr. Newberry pulled out a bag of gingersnaps. "Care for one?"

"Yes, I would. Thank you." She munched on it and sipped her juice. Mr. Newberry gave a gingersnap to Fred.

"I don't diversify much," he said to Kate. "Chairs, stools, a table or two. Now and then I do a cabinet or a chest of drawers. These things bear thinking on, you know."

"Mr. Newberry, I'm an interior designer. Your kind of furniture is just what I'm looking for."

"Is it now?" he boomed, a pleased expression on his face. "In that case, you'd better try out that chair over here. Lean back in it a bit. I like my chairs to be tested. Wouldn't have it otherwise."

The chair *was* comfortable. Kate settled back in it, stretching out her legs. Mr. Newberry went on sanding as his deep voice continued, "Pine. Now, too many people turn up their noses at your basic pine . . ."

Fred plopped down in a corner, his eyes closing. He snored quietly. Kate blinked. Here she was, all relaxed and comfortable, and those blasted tears were starting again. She struggled to her feet. Fred opened his eyes and looked at her in annoyance.

"I have to go now, Mr. Newberry. But I'll be talking to you again about your wonderful furniture."

"Take another gingersnap for the road."

"Yes, I think I will."

She munched on it, blinking furiously, as she crossed the moat again under the baleful stare of the ducks. She hurried to the curb where she'd left her car. San José or Steven's? She put her yellow Bug in gear and chugged her way up the hill. She passed Steven's house, foot pressed to the accelerator.

But it wasn't any use. She felt as if she were bound to him by invisible cords, tugging her toward him. She backed up and pulled into the drive behind the Mercedes. Emerging slowly from her car, she stood against it for a moment. Then she gripped her briefcase and strode up the walk.

Steven was wearing jeans and had his feet propped up on the coffee table in the library. Kate stared at his yellow-and-brown checkered socks.

"Hello," she said. He lowered the sheaf of legal papers he'd been studying and sat up straight.

"Hello there."

"Um, I guess I'll just get to work..." Her eyes weren't leaking anymore, but she had an ache in her chest. Could he ever turn from all the Gloria Nestors of the world and love only her? Could he possibly?

"Sit down. Let's talk," he urged. She balanced herself uneasily on the edge of an armchair and gazed at him. Why did he have to look so devastatingly handsome?

For a while neither one of them said anything. Kate looked at the smear of paint on the sleeve of Steven's shirt; she wondered if he even knew it was there. It was cornflower blue, the same shade as the trim in the upstairs bathroom.

"So, Steven," she began at last, "have you made up your mind yet? About what you're going to do next, I mean. Join the law firm in Los Angeles? Open a practice in a little town somewhere..."

"I haven't decided." He smiled at her. "I'm delaying, just the way you are. Maybe we're more alike than I thought."

"Maybe we feel the same way...about a few things."

"Do you like Marx Brothers movies?" Steven asked.

"Yes . . ." she admitted.

"Do you like organ music at baseball games, and the kids selling hot dogs in the stands?"

"Well, yes—"

"So there you have it," he said. "Already we agree on two major issues. We can always compromise on the rest."

"Steven, there's only one issue that matters!" Kate burst out.

"What's that?" he asked with interest. "Tell me about it."

She sprang up, afraid that she really would tell him. She'd say out loud that any compromise could be reached—if only he loved her. But no, she wasn't going to let herself say it. Being in love with Steven was like being swept away by a tidal wave. She actually felt that she would give up anything—even her independence— to win his love. How could she have allowed this to happen?

She headed for the door like a drowning victim making one last desperate swim toward land.

"Wait!" Steven said. "I want to hear about it. What do you think is the most important issue, Kate?"

"I'm busy," she answered with determination. "I'm going upstairs to work."

"You don't need to work right now."

"Yes, I do."

The phone jangled sharply from the hall. They both made a dash for it, but Kate got there first.

"Hello!"

"Kate, it's Paula. Guess what! I've just made a major breakthrough with Mrs. Cleeve. She invited me to eat lunch at her house today, and we sat on chairs. Real chairs!"

"That's fine," Kate said distractedly. Steven was leaning against the wall next to her, his fingers tracing a path down her cheek.

"I don't think you understand the significance of this," Paula said, her voice squeaking with excitement. "We've reached an agreement! We've decided that two of her rooms will have a Japanese motif—cushions, short tables, the works. But the rest of the house stays French Provincial all the way!"

Kate made an effort to concentrate. Steven's finger had found an extremely sensitive spot behind her ear.

"Paula, this is...wonderful news. I...I knew you'd handle everything...superbly. Does this mean we can finally...." Steven's lips were feathering Kate's left eyebrow. She closed her eyes.

"What's that, Kate?"

"Um, can we expect payment—"

"She promised to write out a check first thing Monday morning!"

"That's good, Paula," she murmured. "That's just wonderful...but I really have to go now. Goodbye." She hung up the phone blindly and rested her forehead against Steven's chest. He massaged her shoulders.

"You're all tense," he said. "Relax. Does that feel good?"

"Oh, yes." His touch was all she craved right now.

"Kate, I talked to Gloria again today. She says that Far Horizon will let you keep the name Melrose Designs."

Kate opened her eyes and stared at the brown plaid of his shirt. How could he be talking about Far Horizon? Couldn't he tell what was happening to her? It was a cataclysm of her entire being. It was a tempest, and he was at the very center of it. Yet he didn't even know.

"That's not all Gloria agreed to," he went on. "She's promised that none of your client consultations will be supervised—not even the ones with Marietta and her niece." He rubbed Kate's shoulders some more. "Loosen up—you're tensing your muscles."

She pulled away from him.

"You picked your moment again, didn't you?" she accused. "You waited until you thought you had me all happy and relaxed, and then you started in about Far Horizon!"

"Dammit, Kate, I'm just trying to negotiate a good deal for you. Gloria's cooperating a lot more than you are. That's pretty ironic, when you think about it. She's being a real professional. Why can't you be one, too?"

Kate grabbed up her briefcase, clenching her fingers around the handle. It made her so angry, the way Steven always compared her to Gloria Nestor and found her lacking somehow. She'd had enough of it.

Suddenly the decision about Far Horizon seemed very simple. Kate wanted to fight Gloria. She needed to fight! Loving Steven was something she could never escape. Very well, then. She wouldn't run away anymore. Instead she would confront Gloria and go to battle for Steven. Far Horizon Enterprises would be the battleground.

A small part of Kate tried to protest, clamoring that this was not the way to make a business decision. She would be using Far Horizon for her own private ends then—just like Gloria. But the protest was swept away by a wave of exhilaration. She had a plan of action now and she needed that more than anything else.

Kate looked at Steven.

"I'll do it," she said. "That's right, I'm going to do it. I'm going to join Far Horizon!"

EVERYTHING WAS ARRANGED quickly and smoothly. Before Kate was ready for it, the big morning arrived. Today she was going to sign a contract with Far Horizon Enterprises.

She woke up with a sense of dread that would not go away. Once again she stood in front of her closet. She needed to wear an outfit that would give her fortitude and confidence. Dresses, pants and skirts flew out of the closet and landed in a heap on the bed. Kate's hair became a wild tumble from pulling clothes on and off. But nothing was right, not even her aqua business suit. Today it only made her look pale and washed out.

She was desperate. Slapping on a pair of corduroys and a blouse, she grabbed her car keys and left the apartment. She ended up on a street of fashionable boutiques that sold everything from jewelry to pipe tobacco. But Kate was on a specific mission, and she singled out the clothing stores. For a long moment she gazed at a dress in one shop window. Then she went inside and asked to try it on.

It was a swirl of amber silk. The material was soft, cool and soothing as it settled against Kate's skin. She turned one more time in front of the shop mirror, then sighed. The dress was beautiful and far too expensive. But for just a moment it gave Kate the illusion that her life was still normal, still her own.

"Looks great," said the salesclerk around her wad of chewing gum. She leaned against a dress rack in her fuchsia miniskirt and her high-heeled black leather boots. "I'll ring it up for you."

Kate glanced around the trendy little store, which charged far too much for its clothes. "What I really need is a skirt," she said. "Something sensible." She went to the racks and pulled out an A-line style that would wear very well. It was khaki. Kate shoved the skirt back into place and found herself in front of the mirror again. The dress was cut in elegant simplicity, with cap sleeves, a V neck and a softly belted waist. The color brought out the gold in Kate's hair and the rose of her complexion.

"Bet your boyfriend would like it," the salesclerk said, chewing her gum.

"I don't have a boyfriend!"

"Then you really need that dress." The girl went to the mirror herself, patting the sides of her spiky black hair. "Of course, if you don't want it, we sell plenty of *boring* clothes. We'd go broke if we didn't. You know what I mean?"

Kate looked at the price tag again and winced. She had been so careful with money lately, determined that never again would she suffer financial bondage to Steven. The dress simply wasn't part of her budget. Of course, once she was working for Far Horizon, she'd be able to afford ten dresses like this. But the idea didn't cheer her at all. What was she getting herself into today? All the money in the world couldn't replace her freedom.

She reminded herself that she was joining Far Horizon for one important reason—to fight for Steven. She couldn't think about anything else, or her resolve would truly waver. The silk material felt like liquid gold in her hands. With such a dress, she could hold her own, even against Gloria Nestor. She turned to the salesclerk.

"I'll take it," she said.

Kate was ready in the amber dress when Steven picked her up at her apartment later in the morning. At first they were tense with each other. But once they were standing in front of the Far Horizon building, Steven took Kate's hand and drew her close.

"You're luminous," he said. "You shine with your own light." His fingers brushed through the flaming curls of her hair. Then he released her gently. "You're going to dazzle them up there," he told her. Ever since she'd announced her decision to him, he had been so excited for her, so proud of her. And she basked in his approval. She was like a planet in orbit around the sun, needing Steven's warmth for her very life.

She walked with him toward the plate-glass doors and her reflection bounced back at her, distorted. She paused, taking a gulp of air. She was doing the right thing. Surely, surely she was doing the right thing. But she didn't have time to ponder any doubts. Her decision to join Far Horizon had gained a momentum all its own. Now it propelled her forward to the elevator and up to the green and khaki world of Gloria Nestor.

"Hello, Steve. Kate, I'm pleased we're going to work together, after all." Gloria was cool and businesslike today. She wore a severe black trench dress, which heightened her dramatic beauty. But Kate didn't let that intimidate her; she looked her best today. She regarded Gloria steadily, and Gloria finally gave a faint smile.

"You've managed to drive quite a bargain for Melrose Designs, Kate. I have to congratulate you on that. Along with everything else, you're getting one of the best offices on the floor. Right across from mine, in fact."

Yes, the office was right where Gloria could keep an eye on Kate—it hadn't been possible to win a concession on all points. But the fight had barely started; Kate didn't expect or even want it to be easy. Her success at

Far Horizon would be all the more triumphant if it was hard-earned. She went with Steven into Gloria's office.

"Steve, are you sure you finally approve of the contract?" Gloria asked in a teasing voice, all her attention now on him. "You're certainly the most thorough lawyer I've ever known."

"I wanted Kate to have the best deal possible," he said mildly. "I'll let her read over the contract for herself now. Go ahead, Kate. Take your time."

Gloria made an impatient gesture, but Kate sat down and read each clause carefully and thoroughly. She had no doubt that she would find everything in order; she just needed to delay signing her name for a few more moments. Surely that was understandable—she was taking a big step.

At last she had to raise her head and nod her acceptance. She picked up a pen and inched it toward the signature line. Gloria's low, throaty voice took over.

"I'm glad we'll have this out of the way now, Kate. Everything is set up for you to meet with Marietta and Brenda tomorrow. But that means we have a lot to accomplish today. Your schedule is typed out for you right here. You'll go to Personnel for briefing, and then you'll meet with another client. I'll give you his folder and I'll expect you to know the contents. I won't be standing over you, but I certainly don't want any more slip ups with our clients."

Kate's pen hovered over the contract. Gloria's voice went on relentlessly. "You'll have appointments this afternoon with two of the vice-presidents. Just look interested no matter how much they drone on—we try to keep them as happy as possible. And at seven you'll meet Amelia Bledloe for dinner. She's very influential

upstairs, Kate, so of course you'll wear something ... suitable.''

The pen froze right on the signature line. Kate took
a deep, cleansing breath and set the pen down.

After listening to Gloria, she understood. If she
signed her name right now, every day of her life she'd
be fighting with Gloria over petty details, over bits and
pieces of time and expenses typed up on a sheet of paper. That was how it would be. Not a grand and
glorious struggle to win Steven's love.

''Is something wrong?'' Gloria asked politely. Kate
looked at her and saw the brittle wariness underneath
Gloria's beauty. Then Kate looked at Steven. His face
was carefully expressionless, but he returned her gaze
intently. She gave a little shrug.

''I'm thinking,'' she said. ''I need some time to think,
that's all.'' She ignored Gloria's grimace of frustration, sat back in her chair and clasped her hands in her
lap. She thought deeply about the reason she had decided to join Far Horizon Enterprises. She had needed
so badly to prove something to Steven, to show him that
she could triumph in Gloria's world. Perhaps she
could ... but she didn't want that kind of success. It
would mean compromising the person she really was.
And no matter how much she loved Steven, she could
not do that for him.

Kate stood up. If Steven was ever going to love her at
all, it would have to be for herself. She didn't belong in
Gloria's world, and could no longer pretend that she
did. This was not a declaration of independence from
Steven. It was simply a calm, strong ability to look inside herself and know what was right for her. Kate felt
that today, for the first time, she had a glimpse of true
independence. It was an action, not a reaction.

"I've changed my mind," she said. "You can't have Melrose Designs."

Gloria's face went cold and hard. "We've bent over backward to accommodate you, Kate. I'm sure you realize that."

"I do. And I'm genuinely sorry to have wasted so much of your time." She picked up her briefcase.

"Just a minute!" Gloria snapped. "You're not going to do this to me, Kate. I've practically kissed the floor for old Marietta because of you!"

"I believe you saw a little profit in it for yourself," Kate said, still calm. "Good day, Gloria."

"I'll sue you for this!"

"Talk to my lawyer."

"Steve, you'd better do something—"

"Sorry, Gloria. My client makes up her own mind." He took Kate's elbow and ushered her to the elevator. The doors glided shut noiselessly and Gloria's outraged face disappeared.

Kate stared at a jade-colored wall. "I know what you must be thinking, Steven. I know how much you disapprove of me right now. But I guess that's just the way it has to be."

Without quite knowing how it happened, she found herself engulfed in his arms. He chuckled. "I'm damn proud of you, Kate Melrose."

"What?"

"Just what I said. I still think you have the worst business habits known to mankind—or womankind, for that matter. But you sure know how to make an exit."

"Steven . . ." she whispered against his chest, closing her eyes. She reveled in the feel of his arms.

"I didn't mean to railroad you, Kate. When you walked out of there, I realized I'd been pushing you too hard about all this."

"I just wanted to make you...like me," she murmured. "That's not exactly the best way to conduct business."

"Kate, don't you realize by now it doesn't matter *what* you do? You could paint my entire house flaming pink and I still wouldn't be able to resist you."

"Oh, Steven—" She couldn't finish, because his mouth had captured hers. He kissed her thoroughly, holding her tight, and she gave herself up joyously to him. It really was possible. It really was possible to be her own independent self and still have Steven close to her.

The elevator doors slid open. Kate and Steven slowly disentangled. She was in a delicious daze.

"Good morning!" Steven called out cheerfully to several amused faces. "Wonderful day, isn't it?"

Kate smoothed the hair back from her flushed cheeks. Steven put his arm around her and propelled her out of the building. "I really didn't mean to force you into anything with Far Horizon," he said. "It just seemed like such a good idea to me. And you did take the place by storm."

"Well, I've been thinking about some of your other ideas, Steven," she said solemnly, "and you're right. Unless I get control of my finances I could lose the freedom my business gives me. I don't want that to happen, and I want to offer Paula and Max something more, too. The first thing I'm going to do is hire an accountant."

"That's fantastic, Kate! A very sound move. I'll get the names of some good accounting firms for you—"

"Hold on, financial adviser. That's it for today."

"All right," he said, conceding. "This is your day, Katie, your celebration. Where to?"

There were so many possibilities. It didn't matter which one she chose, as long as she was with Steven.

"Fisherman's Wharf," she announced. "That would be perfect. Let's go!"

A red kite sailed high in the bay breeze, and fishing boats rocked lazily in the water. The Golden Gate Bridge rose in fiery color against the clear blue sky; beyond was the softer, dusky hue of the Marin hills. Kate thought it was all incredibly beautiful. Though she knew any view would be beautiful to her today, because she was with Steven.

They wandered past stalls of shrimp and crab, breathing in the pungent odors of ocean air and fish. They bought chunks of sourdough bread and seafood cocktails in paper cups, then stopped to watch a puppet show. It was all about a purple dragon who wanted to be an opera singer but couldn't hold a note. Kate hoped everything would turn out all right and the dragon would have his dream of singing at the Met. Steven kissed her, his lips tasting of lemon and salt.

They came to a display of seashell jewelry, watercolors, handwoven wall hangings. Together they picked out a hanging for the house, striped in shades of apricot and rust.

"For the library," Steven said.

"That's exactly what I was thinking." Kate smiled up at him and got another kiss. Hands clasped, they strolled past more stalls and shops.

"Books," Kate said, spying a low doorway and dragging Steven toward it. "That's what we need, books for all those shelves in the library." Inside the small shop she introduced him to the art of dusting off book covers and carefully opening cracked bindings.

"I used to love *Winnie the Pooh*," she said, sneezing into her bandanna. "And look—*Gulliver's Travels*, *Jane Eyre* . . . Here's an author I've never heard of before, but I think we should take all his books. He was very prolific—I like that."

The clerk loaned Kate a big apron to protect her dress as she went squeezing among the grimy shelves. Her pile of books grew to a respectable size, but so far Steven had only decided on one mystery novel. Kate shook her head in disapproval.

"That's not how to shop for books, Steven. You have to get into the spirit of things."

"I made that mistake last time I went shopping with you," he said grimly. He chose one more mystery as his contribution, and watched with a pained expression as the back seat and trunk of the Mercedes filled up with books.

"I love the smell of musty pages," Kate declared. "It promises all those long, satisfying hours of reading. There's nothing quite like it."

Steven coughed and rolled down the window. "Nothing like it," he agreed dryly. They drove up to the house, then carried all the books inside and stacked them wherever they could find an empty space. Kate was glad that she and Steven had the house to themselves. She balanced a copy of *Grimm's Fairy Tales* on the mantel. But today she didn't need any fairy tales. She had her own life. Her own love.

She turned slowly and found Steven watching her from the doorway. At the look in his eyes, her pulse began a slow, sensual beat. She hesitated only a moment, then walked toward him. She would make Steven love her. She had to.

He caught her close, burying his face in her hair. "Kate, maybe I'd better leave right now. I've never seen you look so desirable," he murmured huskily.

"No, Steven," she whispered against his neck. "This is your house, remember? Please don't go."

"Kate, are you sure?"

In answer she lifted her head and claimed his mouth for her own. As she pressed against him, her body ignited with his heat. His hands moved down the length of her back, her hips, caressing her through the silk. With a small, gasping moan she strained closer to him, molding her softness to his strength. Her very soul was inflamed with him.

His kisses grew more demanding, more urgent. Hands twining through the masses of her hair, he arched her face back to his. Her own hands slid down the hard leanness of his back, a rippling response under her fingers. She explored the narrowness of his waist, then moved her hands back up to the breadth of his shoulders.

"Kate . . ." His breath was as ragged as hers, his eyes dark as he gazed down at her. He lifted her into his arms in one powerful motion. Gasping her surprise, she clung to him, burying her face in his neck. Their hearts beat wildly together.

He stood like that for a moment, head bent over hers. Then, arms still tensed beneath her weight, he strode from the room and up the stairs. She wrapped her arms more tightly around his neck and closed her eyes as he mounted each step. Her heart was pounding as if to burst, her breasts crushed against his chest. A moment later he lowered her very gently onto his bed and knelt over her. He smoothed the hair back from her face.

His mouth descended to hers again. His lips bruised hers with sweetness and desire as he turned her body until its entire length was pressed against him. One strong, sure hand moved along her side and his touch burned through the fabric of her dress, but still he wasn't close enough. Kate's blood surged through her veins as he caressed her. She moved so that he could untie the belt at her waist, then draw the loosened dress down over her shoulders.

"You're beautiful...so beautiful," he murmured thickly, his fingers brushing over the smooth, creamy skin of her throat, her shoulders... Her whole body throbbed to him, every nerve exquisitely alive.

"Steven, I love you so much!" The words were out before she could stop them. His hands on her tensed.

"Steven?" she whispered.

"Come away with me, Kate," he said roughly. "Tonight. Tomorrow. Just come away with me."

She buried her head against his shoulder so that he couldn't see her face. "What do you mean, Steven?"

"We can go anywhere you like. I don't know what'll happen, but we can take it one day at a time."

"What will we be? Lovers? Friends?" The words caught in her throat. She closed her eyes tightly.

"Both, Kate. Isn't that enough? Neither of us needs anything more."

"*I* need more, Steven!" she cried from the very depths of her heart. "Please..."

He was silent. She clung to him, willing him to say the words she longed so desperately to hear. Willing him to say he loved her. If he could make that one commitment to her, she'd risk everything—

"I want you so much, Kate."

She closed her eyes even tighter. With one heaving effort she rolled away from him to crouch at the end of the bed. Fingers shaking uncontrollably, she pulled her dress up over her shoulders.

"Darling, what's wrong?" Steven was beside her in an instant, reaching his hands out to her.

"No!" She twisted away from him and backed toward the door, hugging her arms to her chest. Why couldn't he at least say the words even if he didn't mean them? Anything so that she could run back into his arms.

But he said nothing. He stared back at her, his face expressionless. Even in the mellow afternoon light the angles of his jaw and cheekbones were sharpened. He looked harsh and uncompromising.

Kate whirled and stumbled through the hall, down the stairs, and out the door. She looked around frantically for her car, then remembered that Steven had picked her up today. Blast! She ran all the way down to the bus stop, turning to gaze back up the hill. But Steven hadn't followed her.

Late that night Kate huddled in her rocker, wrapped in her flannel robe. She was shivering even though the night wasn't cold. Beside her on a small table of inset porcelain she had propped up the photograph of herself and Steven—locked together in an embrace and yet fighting each other so stubbornly. She stared at the photograph, listening for the telephone to ring. The hours passed in silence.

At last Kate wept, cradling her forehead on her knees. But her racking sobs were no comfort, gave no easing of the deep pain inside her heart.

CHAPTER ELEVEN

"GRACIOUS, I HAVEN'T THOUGHT about any of this in years." Lucy Martin smoothed back a strand of blond-rinsed hair, tucking it firmly into her immaculate chignon. "Yes, I suppose there was quite a scandal before Mama and Papa married," she said in her careful, clipped voice. "Later they were so...settled, you know. Devoted to each other, of course."

"So your father *was* Michael." Kate tried to relax in Mrs. Martin's fussy living room. There were frilly pillows all about, and ruffles around the bottoms of the armchairs and sofa. She felt stifled in here, with the air smelling strongly of carpet deodorizer, but she had to find out about Michael and Eliza. Their story was the lifeline she'd been hanging on to these past few days. If she didn't think about them, she was afraid that the ache in her heart would completely engulf her. It was the unbearable ache of knowing that Steven didn't love her.

"Michael James Hobbes II," said Mrs. Martin. "That's all Papa had—his name and his ambition to be an actor. Not a penny to him. Well, my mother's family was utterly opposed to the match. Grandpa Trimble was making his fortune in department stores, you know. It's all gone now, unfortunately."

Kate leaned forward intently, pushing away one of the fat, frilly pillows that had worked its way under her arm. "About Eliza and Michael. How did they finally convince her family to give in?"

"They didn't." Mrs. Martin crossed her long, thin legs and smoothed her skirt. "They eloped. It was all very romantic. Mama climbed out the attic window—yes, the one in that house you're working on—and nearly broke her neck before she made it down the trellis. The family searched for her, of course, but by the time they found her, it was too late. She was already married to Papa."

"Did he go on acting?"

"All his life. He wasn't terribly successful at it. He wasn't tall or handsome enough to be a leading man with any of the major acting companies. But he was good. Yes, I believe he was quite good. And Mama always encouraged him." Mrs. Martin carefully lined up the rings on her fingers. Kate shifted as another pillow worked its way around her back.

"I'm glad—very glad to know that your parents were happy," she said.

"So am I," Mrs. Martin said with a tinkling laugh that didn't fit her tall, thin frame. "It's not the sort of thing you think about, but it's there, very comforting as you grow up. Would you like to see some family pictures?"

"Oh, yes—please."

Mrs. Martin brought out a leather-bound photo album and dusted it off. "I don't know when I looked at these last. There's Mama and Papa...that's me...my sisters Maggie and Joan..."

Eliza Rose Hobbes had a generous smile and a wealth of dark hair worn piled high on her head. Apparently she hadn't minded the fact that all that hair made her taller than Michael. He was a balding man with a distinctive handlebar mustache, very good-looking in his own way. The two of them smiled out from picture after picture, their love for each other vibrant even through the age-yellowed film. There they were posing on the wharves, biking through Golden Gate Park, glancing at the camera from a dance floor, and Eliza was wearing the burgundy ball gown Kate had found in the attic. The material fell gracefully from her broad but elegant shoulders, then swooped to the floor.

Kate's fingers hovered over the photograph. It evoked a much more recent memory, a magical moment in a hot, stuffy attic.

She perused the rest of the album with determined concentration. Pictures of Eliza's three little girls, playbills from obscure theaters that announced Michael James Hobbes in the roles of Othello or Hamlet or King Henry IV. Then a picture of the whole family with the house in the background. Kate's house, with all the bay windows, the madcap tower, the reckless profusion of gingerbread trim. Only it wasn't her house. It never really had been.

With effort she said, "Did you grow up there? On McClary Hill?"

"Yes," Mrs. Martin said. "The Trimble side of the family came round after a while. When they moved to another place, they left that house for my parents. Mama always loved it."

Kate sighed. "I know how she felt. Thank you so much for your time, Mrs. Martin. Shall I send the boxes and the trunks over to you?"

"Please. I really should go through them. I had no idea they were still around." She shrugged and glanced at her watch. "You must excuse me now. I'm due for a hair appointment, and then my youngest daughter is having her engagement party tonight. So much to do..."

"Yes. Well, thank you again."

Kate walked slowly to her car from Mrs. Martin's bland, ranch-style house in San José. The story of Michael James and Eliza Rose was now complete for her. They had loved each other. With their quiet happiness they had faded away in their children's memories. Even the one brief scandal had been relegated to a dim little nook of the past. But that was as it should be. Their happiness had allowed Lucy Martin and her sisters to grow up healthy, to go on to their own happy and busy lives. That was what real love could do.

Kate drove away quickly, but she couldn't escape her own thoughts. She hadn't seen Steven at all since that disastrous afternoon, for he was never at the house anymore. Kate had been working feverishly with Paula and Max to complete each room.

Her hands gripped the steering wheel. Steven's silence was terrible proof that she'd done the right thing that day. If he cared for her at all, then surely he would not have disappeared so completely, so abruptly from her life.

She wanted to call him. A dozen times during the past few days she had picked up the telephone to dial his office. But what would she say?

Her palm thumped down on the horn, and a startled driver glanced over at her from another car. Her body still flamed whenever she thought of that last day with Steven. And since she thought about it all the time, she was in a dangerous state. The car swerved a little.

What if she'd stayed? That question haunted her. She knew the answer—or at least part of it. She would have become Steven's, completely and irrevocably. But afterward . . .

She had to pull over to the side of the street. A wave of desolation swept over her, so intense that she pressed her hand to her stomach. If only Steven had loved her. Oh, why couldn't he love her?

KATE HAD FINISHED all her work on Steven's house, and she walked through it one last time. The sun room was just as it should be—light and airy, a rocking chair much like Kate's own sitting in front of the rounded windows. The kitchen was cheery, too, with marigold curtains and new checkerboard tile on the floor. Everything was arranged so that Steven could cook omelets with ease.

She quickened her pace as she went out to the hall. In the corner was a magnificent old grandfather clock. She had searched all over for it, making sure it chimed loudly every fifteen minutes. She hurried past it, going up the stairs. Here was the study she'd created for Steven. The carpet was a warm Turkish red, a perfect contrast to the rich gray fabric of the recliner. Shelves had been installed all the way to the ceiling, and held some of the books she and Steven had purchased together. Everywhere she turned there were memories. Down the hall she came to the room where the Monet print hung in a place of honor. She had built the entire room around it, using subtle shades of blue and cloud white. It was a peaceful place, welcoming contemplation, but Kate could find no rest there.

Now she was confronted by the closed door of Steven's bedroom. That was the one room she hadn't even touched. That last afternoon with him, when he

had swept her up and carried her there in his arms—
what had it really meant to him?

She ran downstairs to the library and grabbed her
briefcase. This room, in tones of orange and earthy
brown, was the most inviting of all. The wainscoting
was finished at last, the shelves stocked with the rest of
those musty old books. The decrepit sofa had managed
to retain its place, but looked jaunty in new upholstery.
Above it was displayed the wall hanging she and Steven
had purchased at Fisherman's Wharf.

Everything should have been perfect. Kate had
created a warm, homey atmosphere throughout the
house. It was the sort of place where children should
pound up and down the stairs, dogs should pad through
the hall, a husband and wife should kiss hello and
goodbye at the front door.

Kate gripped the edge of the mantelpiece. She stared
at the neat row of M&Ms lined up along it. With an in-
articulate cry she swept her hand along the mantel,
scattering the candies everywhere.

She fled the house and went straight to Marietta
Winfield's mansion on Nob Hill. Kate was grateful that
she'd been invited for tea; she was seeking any refuge
she could find. Today Marietta's dark, cluttered rooms
offered solace, a retreat from color and life—and
therefore a retreat from pain.

Marietta's silver tea service was enormous and elaborate. The butler had to lean over backward to support
the weight of it, yet he deposited it without a rattle on
the table. He vanished as silently as he had come.

The teapot was awe-inspiring, engraved with a pattern of large grape leaves. Marietta grasped the handle
in both hands and lifted the pot, arms trembling with
the effort. Kate reached out her own hand, but then

lowered it. She waited respectfully as the spout hovered in the air, dipping down at last to splash the tea into the cups.

The sugar bowl was an easier proposition. Kate took the grape-leaf tongs and helped herself to two perfect little cubes. There were bite-size sandwiches with the crusts cut off, miniature jelly rolls dusted in powdered sugar, raisin cookies in shapes of stars, slivers of carrot cake. Arranging a suitable assortment on the plates under Marietta's supervision took a long while. But Kate found herself soothed by the prolonged ritual. For a moment she could believe that taking tea properly was her only problem in the world.

"There, now." Marietta seemed satisfied at last and sat back. Her gray ringlets were caught about her ears with brown velvet ribbons, and her gown was adorned with a frivolous bit of lace at the collar.

"I just wanted to chat today, Kate—may I call you Kate? But I must confess I also have business motives. I still want you to be my interior decorator."

Kate smiled wonderingly over her teacup. "Even after the upset with Far Horizon Enterprises?"

"Most definitely." Marietta took a minute bite of jelly roll, patted her lips with a napkin and went on, "I enjoyed that thoroughly, you know. Brenda was in fits."

"I'm sorry—"

"No apologies needed." She waved her hand. "I haven't felt so energetic in years. You will take me on, won't you?"

"Only as a friend," Kate asserted. "I'll be happy to advise you on your house, and we'll work on it a bit at a time."

"I will pay you exactly what you charge everyone else. No more argument about it. You'll come to tea again," Marietta went on happily, "and you'll bring that nice gentleman, Mr. Reid."

Kate set her cup down with a little clatter. "I—I don't believe so," she stumbled, trying futilely to recover herself. Marietta set down her own cup.

"Dear me, how foolish of me. I didn't realize. Is it very serious, Kate?"

"Yes." The word came out involuntarily. She concentrated on a raisin cookie.

"Does he know?"

"He must!"

"Dear me..."

The two women were silent. Marietta stirred her tea thoughtfully, then spoke again. "I want to tell you something about the man who built this house, Kate. Joseph Winfield—my grandfather. He was one of the Bonanza Kings of the Comstock Lode. He knew how to take silver—just the *idea* of silver—and turn it into millions of dollars in stocks. He was a rascal, but he knew how to live. He knew how to face his fears head-on, even when he was a very old man. I should have been like him, I worshiped him so much. But I was a very timid, very uncertain young girl, Kate. I wasn't brave like my grandfather. Still...I fell in love. That should have given me some courage."

"And it didn't?" Kate asked softly.

Marietta shook her head until the ringlets quivered. "No. And yet I believe he could have loved me. I believe there was a possibility there, if I had known how to grasp it."

"What if you're ready to take the chance," she murmured, "and he's not?"

"I don't know what to tell you. I'm certainly not one who should give advice. But, my dear Kate, make very sure you know whose fear is stopping you. Yours or his. Make very sure. And now have another cookie."

Kate did, then reached over and clasped the old woman's hand. "Thank you—for everything. Cookies and all."

"Then I have convinced you to come to tea—often?"

"Absolutely."

The slender, papery fingers gave Kate's hand an answering squeeze.

"Good. Tell me what I should do with that funny, lopsided lamp. Do you think I might be allowed to keep it? My grandfather was so proud of it..."

"Certainly you'll keep it. But you could put it on a new table if you like. I know just the person to provide it. Mr. Newberry is his name." She smiled, knowing instinctively that Mr. Newberry would get on very well with Marietta. He had dozens of pockets and a beagle named Fred. He would help Kate to bring some light into this house. She didn't want to think about anything else. She didn't want to think about Marietta's words, but they haunted her even as she chatted of lamp shades and curtain fringes. *Make sure you know whose fear is stopping you... make very sure.*

As Kate left Marietta's house, she forced herself to acknowledge her own fear. On her last day with Steven, *she* had been the one to run away. She hadn't been brave enough to stay and take a risk with him. Yes, the risk was monumental; perhaps Steven would never love her. But she had to give him a chance. She had to be with him, doing everything she could to convince him that he *did* love her.

Kate's heart lightened. She was suddenly filled with hope, and she spent the rest of the afternoon foraging through old bookshops. She found the ones hidden away on side streets, ancient signs with faded lettering tacked over their doors. Kate lurked in their dusty aisles, sneezing into her bandanna. She climbed ladders to the highest shelves while clerks hovered anxiously below. She shook her head and climbed back down again. But at last she found what she was looking for.

Very early the next morning Kate drove back up McClary Hill, a package beside her. Heart thumping, she pulled into the drive. This was taking all her courage—more than she really possessed. And yet she knew Marietta was right. She had to face her fears. She had to take a chance. All her happiness depended on it.

But the Mercedes wasn't there. Dew sparkled on grass that was beginning to thrive. Water glinted in the fountain, the stone ship at sail again. The house looked cheerful in its sunny coat of yellow. And a For Sale sign was pounded ruthlessly into the ground in front of it.

"No. No! Dammit, Steven Reid, no!" But he was not there to hear.

CHAPTER TWELVE

KATE WALKED RESTLESSLY back and forth in the office of Horace Dilwood, real-estate agent. What was keeping the man? She was ready to fight out terms with him. She'd need to fight, because she didn't have a down payment for the house. But she was determined to own it. No one could stop her—least of all Steven.

He had left town and couldn't be reached. That was what the real-estate agent had told her, anyway. More than likely Steven just didn't want to be reached. There was nothing she could do about that. But he had abandoned the house and now it was up to Kate to rescue it.

"Come on, Mr. Dilwood," she said impatiently. She spoke in a loud, belligerent voice. The door burst open.

Kate found herself looking straight into Steven's slate-gray eyes. She held on to the back of a chair, willing her heart to calm its absurd pounding. With an effort she tilted her chin. "Why, hello, Steven," she said coolly.

"So it's you," he answered, his voice rough. "I'm sorry, Kate, but I've decided not to sell the house."

Anger blazed through her. "Surely you can see it belongs with me," she declared. "I'm the one who loves it!"

"I'm the one who bought it in the first place," he said. "Don't you think I care about it at all?"

They glared at each other across Mr. Dilwood's desk.

"Frankly, no. I don't think you care in the least."

Mr. Dilwood hovered around them. He buttoned his sweater, then unbuttoned it all the way down.

"Please, please!" he murmured. "I'm sure we can come to a suitable arrangement."

"The house is mine," Kate said, snatching up her briefcase.

"I'm not selling," Steven returned.

"You don't have any choice. I'll—I'll sue you if I have to!"

"I'm your lawyer. How can you sue your own lawyer?"

"Oh dear, oh dear," Mr. Dilwood sputtered, his sweater flapping. "I simply don't know what to say."

"I do," Kate muttered, striding out of the office. "This isn't over yet, Steven Reid!"

Next morning a loud knock sounded at the door of Kate's apartment. She awoke in the cool dawn light and struggled into her robe. Could it be Steven? Please, God—

She yanked the door open, only to find a small boy. "Hello!" he hollered, then shoved an envelope into her hand and ran whooping down the stairs.

Kate tore open the envelope and scanned the single sheet inside. The handwriting was bold, decisive:

WHEREAS, the party of the first part, Steven Reid, does hereby subpoena the other party of the first part, Katarina Melrose, to appear posthaste at the yellow house on McClary Hill.

She leaned against the door, clutching the sheet in one hand and wiping away her tears with the other. Then she smiled. Steven thought he could commandeer her again, and this time he was right. She hurried to the bedroom, slipping into jeans and her favorite flowered shirt. She brushed out her hair and tried to dab on some mascara. The job was thoroughly botched, and she had to start all over again. At last she was ready, and ran out to her car.

When she got to Steven's house, she found him waiting by the mantel. He regarded her solemnly.

"Hello," he said.

"Hello."

"Do you think we can work this out?"

"We can try." Her voice shook, and she turned away quickly.

"Kate... I have something for you."

She was forced to look at him again. He held out a little white sack. It was filled with M&Ms.

"Oh, Steven..."

The bag was crushed between their bodies.

"Tell me what I have to do," he pleaded huskily against her ear. "Because I'll do anything. I can't live apart from you. That's all there is to it, Kate."

She pressed her face against his chest. "Just be here with me."

"I love you, Kate."

She looked up at him in joy. "I love you, too, Steven."

It was a long while before he lifted his mouth from hers.

"You taste like ginger." He kissed one eyebrow, the tip of her nose. "Aren't you going to share those M&Ms?"

She rescued the crumpled bag. "Always."

Steven led her to the sofa. Kate sat beside him, head nestled blissfully against his shoulder.

"My Katie..." he murmured, stroking her hair. "If only you knew... Well, I'll admit it. You scared the hell out of me that day you said you loved me. I'd done such a good job all my life convincing myself I was meant to be a bachelor. For a long time I was even a happy bachelor, Katie. It was easy not to fall in love. The women I knew were like Gloria—successful but always driven. Always looking for more success, never knowing when to stop and just enjoy life a little. I could understand that, of course—I was like that myself for such a long time. But then you burst into my life, with all your colors and flowers."

She pressed herself closer to him. "I'm here to stay," she said.

"You'd better be." He held her tightly. "I think I've loved you since that very first day. There you were, trying to hide your delectable body in that business suit..."

"Oh, it took me a little longer to fall for you," she said mock-seriously. "It wasn't until I saw you in a bath towel."

He chuckled, then ravished her mouth again. She clung to him, feeling decidedly unsteady. Steven traced the line of her widow's peak with his finger.

"I kept trying to fight my love for you, Kate. You were shaking up my entire life, and I resisted as long and hard as I could. I flew out to Vermont last week. I thought if I got away from San Francisco, I'd be able to see things more clearly. I saw them, all right. I saw what a damn fool I'd been—afraid to admit I loved you. I guess all along I'd known that you were the only woman who could change my life—deep down, where it really mattered. That was pretty damn scary."

"Oh, Steven, I was afraid, too. I thought loving you meant losing all my freedom. But now I know I can't be free without you."

"You'll never lose your independence with me, Katie. All I want is to share my life with you—right here in San Francisco. This is where I'm going to have my new practice in family law."

Kate drew back so that she could look at him.

"Steven, that's wonderful!" she exclaimed. "I'm so happy for you. I'm so happy for both of us! But I almost forgot—I have a present for you, too."

The book was bound in old leather, its gold tooling chipped and faded. Steven turned the yellowed pages carefully.

"*The Adventures of Sherlock Holmes*." He grinned. "My favorite. How did you know?"

"Elementary, my dear Steven."

"I'm very glad I'm going to marry you, Katie. You *will* marry me, won't you?"

"Yes. Oh, yes."

He kissed her again, tenderly.

"This old house needs us," he said. "We can't let it down, can we?"

"No, we can't," she answered softly. His arms enfolded her. There were no barriers to keep her from him now. She was home at last.

Six exciting series for you every month... from Harlequin

HARLEQUIN
Romance®

The series that started it all

Tender, captivating and heartwarming...
love stories that sweep you off to faraway places
and delight you with the magic of love.

◆

Harlequin Presents®

Powerful contemporary love stories...as individual as the women who read them

The No. 1 romance series...
exciting love stories for you, the woman of today...
a rare blend of passion and dramatic realism.

◆

Harlequin Superromance®

It's more than romance... it's Harlequin Superromance

A sophisticated, contemporary romance-fiction
series, providing you with a longer,
more involving read...a richer mix of complex plots,
realism and adventure.

HARLEQUIN

Romance®

Delight in the exotic yet innocent love stories of
Harlequin Romance.

Be whisked away to dazzling international capitals ... or
quaint European villages.

Experience the joys of falling in love ... for the first
time, the best time!

Six new titles every month for your
reading enjoyment!